To Rya

Congratulations and I hope you enjoy the read.

Tony

Peachstone Black

First published in 2015 by
Longmead Publishing.

© Anthony Michael Cornish 2015

Anthony Michael Cornish has asserted his right to be identified as the author of this Work in accordance with the Copyright, Design and Patents Act 1988.

All rights reserved. No part of this publication may be reproduced, stored in a retrieval system, or transmitted in any form or by any means, electronic, mechanical, photocopying, recording or otherwise, without the prior permission of the copyright owner.

Cover image © Mark Chadwick, *Fluid Painting 58*, Acrylic on Canvas 2012

www.markchadwick.co.uk

ISBN 978-0-9932922-0-0

LONGMEAD
publishing

www.longmeadpublishing.com

For Beth

By the same author:

In Search of the Pearl Unique

A glossary of terms and phrases
used in this novella can be found
on the relevant page at:

www.longmeadpublishing.com

Peachstone Black

or

the Thirteenth Labour
of Aloysius Amerigo
Beade, Artist.

by

ANTHONY MICHAEL CORNISH

Cavaliere,

The dreams linger through my waking hours. No, not dreams, but nightmares—terrible and beautiful all at once, full of rage, fire and blood. They tear me open, leave daylight scars, and remake me in their image. They've set the course of my life.

My father was a violent man. It wasn't his beatings of me, but his brutality to my mother that drove her to make an end of herself, then me to make an end of him. The world is a happier place for his absence. The next I murdered by accident, as you will see.

I'm two sides of the coin: Artist first and foremost, dark instrument second. The world's a tawdry, violent place and the Artist's first duty is to translate onto canvas the rare flickers of beauty still to be found this side of life's horizon. My Work's incremental, each fragment a revelation in itself, and the apogee of this miracle will cut you to the quick.

Wicked seed has been sown, but you, Cavaliere, set the wheels of all that followed grinding into motion.

An hour after meeting you, my blood well and truly up, I made a solemn determination: I'll bring you down; humble you; smash into pieces the pedestal upon which you stand preening before the world. I'll place my foot on your neck and push down hard, but from now until then I'll be the worm lodged in your ear, the subtle knife twisting in your side. Stars will fade to black and your world will smoulder. You'll sniff at the corrupted air, bemused, and wonder how things can have plummeted down, down as far as this. How can it possibly be that you, the distinguished Latin nobleman, untouchable and long in the habit of success, pitted his wits against this anarch and inexplicably lost the war? I'll chip away at your carapace; chip, chip, chip. I'll reduce you. Among a tribe of brutes I'd be thought brutish.

But will I ever be truly appreciated? I can but hope. And you must take responsibility for much of what followed, Cavaliere. Sophia, your radiant girl, was a painted butterfly while you can only ever be a moth.

Both brush lightly, wing on skin, but she's all beauty while you're steadfast drab.

Do you recall our first meeting? No? For shame! We were introduced at the Theatre Royal Haymarket, recently made patent and altogether too full of itself. The reek of snuff, perfume and pretension hung heavy in the air. Was it our surroundings that made you decline to shake my hand? Perhaps you mistook me for a tradesman—*I am no mere painter, Sir!*—but when you repeated your error at Enderby, gaffe became insult.

But let's return to the Theatre Royal. You appeared puzzled that we were even inhaling the same air and then grew flustered by my polite bow; a gesture that you did not—*would not?*—reciprocate. You disobliged me. It's one thing to entertain a private prejudice, Cavaliere, but then you played the scene up, up, up to the gallery; the Latin temperament's much given to showing off. I watched them all snickering behind their hands; everyone was drawn into the comedy. True, I've fallen on thin times and my clothes are a little passé, but had you possessed even a modicum of good manners, had you met decency with decency, then our conflict might well have died there and then. Serendipity, I suppose. But later you would compound your insult, feigning interest in my methods, enquiring as to how certain pigments are produced and what use I might then make of them.

Later again, in the course of a fretful night, I turned the trouble over and over in my mind until my anger grew Leviathan. There was no retreat after that. After that you stood condemned. Once past that line in the sand, had you fallen to your knees, begging for my mercy, I would have spat in your eye; I would have pissed upon you, Cavaliere.

5.

The seventh day of January
in the year of Our Lord 1775.

Today we're enjoined to celebrate the life of Saint Raymond of Peñafort. He craved seclusion, but then proved spectacularly ill suited to the hermit's life. Unfortunately, he then redirected his energies into the life literary and penned the dullest tome imaginable on the subject of—can you guess?—penitentiary discipline. This would prove to be his sole legacy. Much better that he'd striven harder to be a worthy Anchorite, lost himself to the world and spared us all that followed.

Cavaliere,

In September of last year I received an invitation from my generous—and most generously moneyed—patron Lord Eustace Wynne Halebroke, requesting my presence at his sumptuous Kentish estate. How could I possibly refuse, never mind that my soul roiled at the thought of gripping his sweating hand in mine to reassure him of my enduring friendship? Then again, after swallowing down the London fog for too long the prospect of a little country air much appealed.

Kabalos insisted that he accompany me. I reluctantly assented, not having any real choice in the matter. He promised to keep himself entirely secret and observe everything. Thus were the events to come set in train.

Lord Eustace Halebroke, quite the stupidest of men, is perversely blessed with unnaturally good luck. He's able to claim scant provenance for his wealth: his thoroughly English predecessors profited from the enclosure of a large portion of Wales, rearing thousands of compliant sheep in the place of a few hundred, infinitely less convenient, boorish tenants. He then had the good fortune to discover that beneath his flocks of sheep lay an abundance of coal. After that his ambitions knew no bounds. Untethered, he purchased the Enderby estate and set about spreading his largesse far and wide, except he can't seem to do so quickly enough to prevent the filthy lucre piling up faster than ever!

So what to do with such a great heap of gold? He purchased, at outrageous expense, a commission into a reputable marching regiment for one of his sons—the younger, or the elder, I neither know nor care—and the second—*or was it the first?*—fruit of his loins has embarked on a truly stellar career. Can you guess at his chosen occupation? Has he gone for a politician, or perhaps a Methodist clergyman to gratify his mother? No, and no again: he's a dissolute gambler, and a remarkably inept one at that. This famously unlucky roué, this young-blood obsessed with wine, women and debauchery, has accrued truly crushing losses at the tables, but even this has failed to stem the indecent tide of money pouring into the family coffers.

To add insult to injury Lord Halebroke's wife, the Lady Margaret, is a relentlessly pious, timid little creature, stricken to have been so elevated above her commonplace beginnings. She's all-too happy with last years' fashions, or even those of the previous year and simply refuses to indulge herself. I expect the day will soon come when the dowdy little thing simply fades to grey, disappears into the ether and draws no further attention down upon herself. She refuses to overcome her longing for country parsimony and refuses to lend her profligate husband a helping, spendthrift hand!

I, however, am enthusiastic to assist Milord in any way I can. I'll put his money to excellent use. At some time in life all men need an escape from the mundane and Lord Halebroke's mad for diversion. Oh, and elevation. Yet the salient thing that Eustace fails to appreciate is this: the society he so fervently aspires to join is almost without exception utterly bereft of funds. Thus, his prodigious wealth, far from providing an easy admission fee, produces quite the opposite effect; in fact, he's jealously despised, but lacks the wit to comprehend the contempt in which he's held.

Milord Halebroke's also grown over fond of certain soft indulgences, by which I mean girl-whores, boy-whores, fine wines, the more superior brands of snuff, silk waistcoats, exotic substances, and all the other trappings of wealth. All this, and yet he never misses an opportunity to loudly proclaim his Methodism and refuses touch a single a drop of alcohol.

His foremost pleasure's the collection of "interesting acquaintances" of all professions, shapes and sizes. Beyond that he expends a stupendous fortune on works of art—very often my own pieces. In this way Aloysius Amerigo Beade is placed, de facto, among Milord's theatre of curiosities. Furthermore, judging by his clammy palms, he's also fallen a tad in love with me. Let me be clear: by this I mean that he covets my person while barely understanding my art. Should his peers ever learn of his inner desires, can you imagine the displays of self-righteous disgust?

There are other men who think of me this way, inhabiting a shallow, infantile world in which golden locks, a fair face, a measure of genius, a modicum of learning and a dose of wit are sufficient to charm the universe. Oh, would that I were older, uglier and set free of it all!

As for his lofty title, this derives from a well-timed loan he extended to an impecunious Royal Treasury, thus enabling the prosecution of this or that foreign war. Was his money expended in the American colonies, or in the defeat of the evil Maratha in faraway India? He neither knows nor cares for in this way he has transmuted his band of surly tenants into mountains of coal, and then his coal into muskets. What a thoroughly modern alchemy: mutton into *matériel*. Rumour has it that the interest rate placed upon the ten thousand pounds in question was preposterously low, but then "interest" can be repaid in so many creative ways. Do you take my meaning?

I travel to Enderby in Milord's private coach, a whirlicote, no less. I go in great style and comfort and slumber through the journey and—*what joy!*—wake to find representatives of all English society there to greet me. Here stands, rather limply it must be said, a poet: a wistful, deathly-pale, ethereal fellow who would surely evaporate if over-exposed to the sun's rays. He also complains incessantly of headaches. There sits a well-known theologian: a remarkably dull, canting little fellow with nothing to offer in conversation beyond a stubborn, imitative set of cod philosophies. Then I encounter a brace of wide-eyed, lackwit politicians, each harbouring pretensions to Milord's patronage and thereafter the very same post in government, thus guaranteeing us a deal of spiteful comedy. Here stands a designer of gardens who'll speak of nothing above plants, trees, herbs and the various blights that so cruelly afflict his leafy darlings. Oh, and over there loafs a chinless, moustachioed, monosyllabic colonel of the very regiment in which Milord's son holds his ill-gotten commission. But finally, here stands a Florentine diplomat dispatched by the Habsburgs to attend the Court of Saint James. Holding yourself aloof from the chitchat I see you: the Cavaliere Ereditario Riccardo Francesco di Credico.

Self-assured, an actor commanding his stage, you glide across the room as if suspended on invisible wires. Without uttering a single word you declare yourself among the worthiest of men, a patrician past equal and in this present company by absolute right. Each languid gesture, the way you hold your head, the arch of an eyebrow, the length of your stride, are all most carefully calculated. You stand tall, a full head above the crowd, statesmanlike and blessed with a most lordly demeanour.

This is our second meeting and this time I'll not bow. Instead, I push back my shoulders and steady my look. In the face of such defiance I watch your mask slip, just a little. Is all that I first believed fact perhaps façade? Is your character not chiselled out of the same Italian marble as your features? We converse politely and I discover a vital thing: you, my self-appointed censor, may very well be accomplished in diplomacy, but it becomes abundantly clear to me that you're not at all well read. Here's a deficiency that no amount of breeding can redress. I scent weakness.

Yes, I'm still referring to you, Cavaliere.

We eat, we drink and the next day venture forth to inflict a bloody carnage by systematically slaughtering innocent, unsuspecting game birds in unnatural numbers. Despite my facility with firearms I'm appalled by the unalloyed savagery and perform badly. A favoured few specimens are devoured later that evening, washed down with a truly unspeakable hot, spiced wine. I loathe guns and the murder of guiltless animals— I prefer larger game—but then a tempting idea elbows its way into my mind: I will arrange a little sport of my own.

Among Milord's serving girls is a pretty, generously proportioned girl; appealing in that charming, countrified way of things. She also displays a comedic propensity to flush blood red at the slightest provocation. It's conspicuously clear that I hold scant attraction for her, so this presents me with my first proper challenge of the evening; a gauntlet's hurled down. No, more of a silken glove drifting listless to the floor. In spite of my rather worn appearance—I've lately been a touch down on my luck—my station in life's as much elevated as hers is resolutely humble, as commanding as hers is to be commanded. She's mine from the first, but remains improperly aware of the proper way of things; she's an unfilled vessel; a simple, unlettered, forest-born nymph in sore need of an education.

Another day brings us fresh opportunities to savage the local wildlife, but by this time my blood's well and truly up and I bag a good many. I'm vigorously clapped on the back and applauded. No such plaudits for Milord: he's every bit as hopeless as before, sweating like a horse as he liberally blasts away.

Milord's social cataclysm of the day comes towards the end of the shoot when a magnificent peacock climbs laboriously into the air and flies along the line of guns as if to flaunt his immunity from the present violence. Each man lowers his weapon as the bird trundles across his line of fire, but not Milord Halebroke. Oh, no: he discharges his piece and for once strikes his target. The peacock strikes the ground with a great, earth-trembling thud. Unaware of his profound error Milord hollers and hoots like a child, applauding his own success while the other guns sneer and struggle—*most unconvincingly*—to conceal their *Schadenfreude*.

Later that evening I ring on the bell and require a restorative flask of wine to be carried up to my room. I also insist that the aforementioned forest nymph be the one to attend me. Once the door's firmly closed behind her she's persuaded to take a cup of wine with me and, true to the greedy nature of the lower castes, quaffs it like beer. I don't doubt she regularly helps herself to one or two leftover glasses and has acquired a taste. I'm fascinated by her rude manners: she gulps down the mixture of wine, powdered coca leaf and other, secret ingredients. She swallows hungrily, detecting nothing untoward; her palate's untutored and insensible to the presence of additives. I mean her no real harm, intending only simple rapine, but as Paracelsus once said *"All things are poison and nothing is without poison; only the dose permits something not to be poisonous".*

'Walk in the privy-garden with me, Mary,' I drawl, wet-lipped and fast-breathing. 'A little air before bed ... fine evening ... dry underfoot ... health-giving.'

Blah, blah, blah.

'But sir!' says she. Most prudent, but even as she slurs the words her desires come, calling up to her, from the lower belly. The objection's hardly past her lips when she stands and shrugs her way into her shawl to defend against the autumn chill. We tiptoe our way through the creaking house, along hall and down stair. Passing through the *allée* and into the arbour I guide her to a secluded place in Milord's—rather woeful—interpretation of a sacred grove. You may hazard a guess at what ensues, but know that none of it's precisely my fault; the silly girl's recklessly provocative. This is how it went from the first:

'Mary,' say I, lust falling from my eyes like dew, 'you know, of course, that I'm an artist of ... well ...'

'Yes, sir?'

'... some standing. Your Master's commissioned a set of works to adorn the walls of his Long-room. Twelve large canvases in total, so now I have a pressing need for comely girls to pose for me.'

A prolonged pause, before the sound of a penny ... slowly ... dropping. The girl's comically dull-witted.

'You surely cannot mean me, sir!'

'And why not, dear girl?' say I, brim-full of purpose. 'I won't dwell on the deficiencies of your class, but will only say this: I see before me a pretty face, a shapely leg ...'

'Pretty, sir? You honestly think me pretty? The truth, now?'

'Indeed! Of course! And such a delightful shape! Your smile's enough to erase any flaw, much like a ... well, who knows what? Too few of my subjects are as perfect as you, dear girl, so will you oblige me?'

'O-oblige you, sir?'

Suspicion. Alarm. I've chosen the wrong word, mistaken which colour to apply from the palette, but then rally in force:

'Perhaps you'll first o-oblige me by not echoing back at me every word that falls from my lips, Mary.'

There it is! Obfuscation! Diversion! And most deftly done! The serving classes are easily cowed by displays of authoritarian confidence; small rebellions quashed without a single cavalry sabre withdrawn from its scabbard. I follow this with a carefully measured pause and then ...

'Perhaps you lack courage.'

'Oh no, I have plenty of that, sir, and to spare. My father's told me so himself.'

I feign indecision, until ...

'I'll pay you, and generously.'

A bite, and then she's my fish-on-a-line.

'Will you do this for me, Mary?'

'Oh! That must surely depend on what you ask of me.'

No coquettishness this time, but rude suspicion. I move quickly to forestall her doubts:

'Can you imagine, err ... Mary ... what my Work demands of me? The daily sacrifice?'

Witness the cleverness with which I lead her along! See how wilfully she follows, the dear-heart? She pauses, pondering for the longest, moonlit moment while my concoction roils in her blood, playing on her reactions and dulling her wits further still.

'I've seen paintings, sir.'

'Indeed.'

'Yes, sir, but will ... will you require to paint my ... well, my shape, sir?'

'Your shape, Mary? What can you possibly mean by that?'

Colour surges to her face; a most becoming flush of embarrassment.

'I suppose, I mean, my, well ... my ... bubbies, sir?'

"Bubbies"? Oh, the dear! A little low comedy, the comedienne unwitting, yet here's the very moment for which I've baited and waited. I strike a studied, disarmingly serious pose, calculated to inspire unconditional trust in weak minded.

'Yes, I see, but now you've raised the matter I'm obliged to answer you in complete honesty. They must, of course, be shapely—I'll never be induced to paint dugs—never in life! So, are your breasts, well, sufficient to the task in hand? Is your shape ... shapely enough to complement my Work, Mary?'

'I ... I don't know, sir. How can I answer such a question for myself?'

The look of shy pride in her eyes tells me that she, at least, believes them pretty enough to launch a ship or two.

'Has your lover never spoken of them? I must know! Does he compare you to ... a cow? I mean, are they dugs? Slung low, like this? Or rather, and this would be so much the better for me, does he see you as ... as Aphrodite reborn?'

She looks blankly at, and then past me. Too theatrical! Too highbrow! I'm losing her. I can overreach.

'I'm asking if they're, well, pert.'

She's offended from several directions at once, but defends herself from only one:

'Lover? I have no lover, sir! I'm much too young to have a lover!'

'Then you're a virgin?'

I ask this matter-of-factly, with pace, and I'm rewarded with another, seductive, vermillion blush. She's a little peach—a decidedly curious, ripe little peach. Thus encouraged I press home my assault:

'Then I must adjudicate the matter for myself. Don't you see how this must be? I have a professional reputation to maintain, Mary; I'm most protective of it.'

She hesitates, but not over-long, before peeling away layer after grubby layer of her clothing to reveal, at tiresome length, the form beneath. I regret that what's on display may only be described as average, or perhaps a little over that. Youthful, certainly, but certainly no Aphrodite, with one or two inconvenient blemishes for my imagination to brush over. And yet she's insufficiently bovine to quieten my manly pulse and this seals the matter. She regards me, regarding her, and raises a quizzical eyebrow, unmistakeably coy this time and, I determine, hardly the innocent she'd have me believe.

I feign appetence, breathing heavily, eyes aglow:

'Mary! They're … well, truly excellent! Astounding! Heavenly! I simply must paint them; immortalise your form in oils! Deny me and I'll very likely become gloomy, then perish alone and unhappy!'

I take up charcoal and paper and set on, all the time feigning an attempt at serious work. Pleasure glows beneath that red-cheeked embarrassment, the airling; a little flattery and she's stricken thoughtless; her gestures all a-pit-pat. I know one certain thing in life: every girl yearns for her womanhood to be immortalised in its prime. What a pleasant game this is! Thus encouraged I press home my advantage:

'Oh, but will this be all for nothing? What do I know of the rest of you? I can only represent my subjects from head to toe and then most faithfully, do you see? My reputation's balanced on a pinhead and my patron, your Master, will doubtless expect ...'

A look of blank incomprehension passes over her features like Venus transiting the face of the sun. I begin to grow impatient:

'The rest, Mary: you must show me the rest.'

Hesitation! Delicious agony! But then she disrobes, horribly clumsily. In her defence she's but eighteen—or thereabouts—and can know little of how to properly entertain a man. You may guess at what follows—I'll spare you the unnecessary details—but I have her there, in the garden, beneath the overhanging oak, amid owl pellets and fungi, to the creak and groan of the old-bone branches spread high above our heads. She warms quickly to her task. Such is the nature of country girls: they're surrounded, and then absorbed, by baseness from birth. At the very moment of ecstasy she, suddenly remote from her situation—her station—promotes me into a higher sphere. She has a rare and unexpected talent.

I'm spent. I'm inspired, but then calamity: the dose administered via her wine—and this I much regret—proves excessive. Too late I realise my error: I calculated her a tad heavier and she dies. My little English rose fades all too soon; she wilts and lies limp. Exhausted, I leave her there, among leaf-mould and droppings and retreat to the sanctuary of my rooms.

We all dwell in our secrets, Cavaliere, every one of us. The secret boy becomes a secretive man. In fact, Mary's end was a beginning. In the months to come there will be other finales, each one uncovering a fresh slice of the mystery of me. As to my sketches of her, none of them will be rendered in oil; I was over excited and unusually clumsy in the execution. They burn.

Come morning, come the furore. Although brief, it's most entertaining. The conversation at breakfast is predictably enervated, and in pursuit of more mischief I mischievously nudge things along as and when I can. The assembly's all a-clamour for details, not least the base. Even after one night her remains have lost what little prettiness they once possessed; how quickly the body turns upon itself once the vital spark's departed. Hedge-animals have also been at her, Master Reynard notwithstanding.

Nota Bene—my considered advice to the secretive man is this: when mired neck-deep in guilt never hurt your own defence by skulking about in fear, head hung low, red-faced and nervous. Avoid nothing. Confront things head on. Protest the loudest among the crowd and put up a veritable storm of indignation. Grow red-faced, enraged, should anyone so much as question you. Shout your alibi from the high mountaintop and defy anyone to demand it of you a second time. Better yet, make casual mention of an incriminating little something, but only the slightest something, lest you butter the bread too thick. Conceal yourself in plain sight.

The mood in the room alters markedly as a latecomer joins our little society. And why late? He's been busy, hard in pursuit of justice, self-appointed sleuth, snooping about the gardens and prodding at the corpse! He speaks, sotto voce, so immediately commanding the avid attention of everyone present. We learn that he's much intrigued by all that he's witnessed. He makes his pronouncement in between stuffing his mouth with a gargantuan breakfast of bacon, poached eggs, devilled kidneys, chops, kedgeree and more, vigorously hacking at his food as if it's somehow offended him. His tone's as resolute as that of the best tub-thumping politician declaiming his manifesto at the stump.

Once the dual trials of his manners and heavy accent are overcome we discover this: he considers himself duty bound to uncover the circumstances of the girl's death. He trumpets his proclamation to the world, but his eyes rarely shift an inch away from mine; he knows me, and all the things I've done. No matter: he'll discover nothing of substance: Paracelsus' philtre is undetectable by now. In any case, I'll be well on my way before he can press the matter further.

Yes, you see me for exactly what I am, quite as readily as I come to know you. We mutter our unspoken vows there, one to the other, over the breakfast table: you'll move heaven and earth to see that I answer with my life for the girl's murder. In reply I vow to preserve myself by keeping that vital inch beyond your reach. I'll make a game of it, allowing your fingertips to brush my coat, but never let you close enough to take firm hold. Why? Not to simply preserve my life, but for the sport! Life's become tiresome of late and the contest will be welcome; a heady spice. More than this, I'll complete my Labours—my Work. From that moment you, the Cavaliere Eriditario Riccardo Francesco di Credico of Florence and Rome and I, Aloysius Amerigo Beade, were joined until End Times.

Our present entertainment's regrettably short lived: a girl of Mary's station will never command the attention of the higher social orders for long. Soon enough the discussion around the breakfast table wilts and then turns to planning the day's sport, by which I mean yet more noisy blasting away at the local wildlife with powder, ball, hallooing, backslapping congratulation and other such nonsenses. It's a complex social ritual and must be observed in detail. The English are a curious race.

My Work. My Labours. I've told you nothing of them, so let's put that to rights. As you know, Milord Halebroke, my noble patron, is only lately come by his elevated status. He and his descendants are bound to endure sneers and be considered vulgar forever.

They're doomed to endure much snickering from behind ladies' fans and be reminded of their rustic origins for at least a century to come.

I recall that his family originated in Halifax, but where in heaven's name is that? One hot summer's day I saw him, quite alone apart from a servant, on the terrace in his gardens. He was sitting in the most ridiculously ornate, throne-like chair, pipe in hand, surveying his estate and sweating heavily in his heavy coat. He's an appalling little man for oh, so many reasons, not least his tendency to excessive perspiration. He is, however, generous with money and would purchase me body and soul if he can. He's a fool for that alone.

Come the third day of this enchanting, country sojourn Milord summons me—rather peremptorily, I must say—into his library. His intention is to describe his plans for me in exhaustive detail. The room's walled, floor-to-ceiling, with leather-bound volumes, I'll wager not one of which he's actually read, nor will likely ever bring himself to do so. They might as well be magnificently bound sheaves of blank paper. Perhaps they are. In fact, has he ever read anything of gravity? His mangled version of English brings me to my conclusion: Seneca knew his ilk: *vita sine litteris mors est*. So, in this shrine to the death of intellect, this celebration of the witless nouveau riche, this cathedral of ignorance, Halebroke lays out his stratagem: he means to employ me to decorate the walls of Enderby's Long-room and thereafter bask in its reflected glory. He means to hear my Work—and therefore his patronage—lauded to the skies the length and breadth of Kent.

'I must have the best, Mr. Beade. Only the most superior of paintings may hang upon my walls. My Long-room must be appreciated throughout the county. Will you oblige me? And in good time? In time for the Christmas festivities? No, no! Not this year! The next, of course! I believe you will succeed, Aloysius, for I've come to regard you as a friend.'

Friend? The prig! The self-righteous, impossible little prig! Worse still, does he take me for a painter of walls and ceilings? Little above a common tradesman? Damn it I'm an Artist! And after December next year he'll no doubt ask me to turn my hand to gardening and have me dig him a ditch or two. Or erect a folly to celebrate his folly? But for now am I able to approve the venture, while nevertheless despising the motive? I mouth a private "yes"; we must all eat and drink and my palate clamours for fine things. Milord has already assumed my acceptance.

As he drones on my imagination trips along like this: in the realms of antiquity Heracles is dispatched, at the command of the fickle King Eurystheus, into the world to perform ten tasks—his Labours—as penance for the brutal slaying of his wife Megara and their children in a cataclysmic fit of rage.

Lord Halebroke believes himself a classicist, sophisticate and scholar, but in truth knows bare fragments of that upon which he pontificates. He will insist on referring to "Hercules", ignorant that his *persona* was borrowed from the Greek "Heracles". Our esteemed Milord is a lumpen, witless pug. I nevertheless warm quickly to the challenge and convey the gist of my inspiration. He readily agrees that I should carry out a series of paintings, each representing a Heraclean Labour, in return for a most handsome fee. The remuneration will be most welcome. As I say, all men must eat and I intend to eat well.

A question for you, Cavaliere: how is it that God sees fit to cross the palm of simple tradesmen and farmers of Halebroke's ilk with silver—and liberally so—while men of genuine quality want for the comforts properly due to men of their class? I deserve comfort, silver and gold. There's precious little virtue to be found in starving to appease one's muse, so I accept Milord's commission, as I must, but with one essential proviso:

'My lord, I declare myself in your debt. Such a great honour! I assure you that my abilities and my person are equal to the task and vow that you'll not be disappointed with my Work.'

'I don't doubt any of that, my dear fellow. I hear you are much admired in London.'

'Indeed, but for such a noble undertaking you will surely understand that I must draw my inspiration directly from the Masters.'

'Indeed? Who are they? I will send for them at once! But will they come here to Enderby, do you think?'

He visibly glows—no, he sweats—at the thought of adding them to his "collection".

'You misunderstand me. Perhaps my English is poor. I refer to the Greek and Roman Masters.'

'Oh, them! I'm sorry, Aloysius, but I believe them long since dead.'

I pause, pray earnestly for grace, and then attempt to enlighten him thus:

'Indeed, sir, the Masters to whom I refer did indeed pass from the world long ago, but their legacy endures in Rome and Florence: statuary, sculpture, architecture, paintings and the air itself. Allow me to play the antiquary and I'll make your Long-room the envy of the county—nay, the entire country—but to do so I must contemplate the works of the Greek and Roman artists and sculptors with my own eyes. I must drench myself in their influence and rediscover my classical muse.'

I intend more than this, of course: much more. I consider it only fair, Cavaliere, that I redress the imbalance in our respective abilities and play out our little game on your native soil. This ought to give you every advantage, if you have the wit to grasp the opportunity.

My esteemed patron swells up like a cockerel, basking in this fresh opportunity to demonstrate his beneficence; spread wide his largesse. Men of Halebroke's sort are all too anxious to inflict their generosity upon the world, bestowing it indiscriminately first here, then there, inflating themselves in the eyes of others. While a boy I was presented with a preserved fish, I think from Greece or thereabouts, quite ugly and puffed up like a spiny cushion: Milord has the same look; all pomp and show, no substance in his bluster and no nip in his spines. He's altogether loathsome.

'Then you must take yourself to Greece and Italy, Mr. Beade. Ah, foreign travel! How I wish I were younger! Why, I might trot along with you and see them for myself!'

God forbid!

'So for you, Aloysius, Rome and Florence it must be! And without delay! But, I fear neither of those places will you find in Greece. Someone has gravely misled you. I have my globe and here lies the first and the second ... just ... there. Both of them lie in Italy! Do you not see? Then look closer. Closer!'

He prods an insistent, pudgy finger, demonstrating the location of first one city then the second. I bend forward obediently, nod, and feign revelation. Later, having explained—affecting a patience I do not feel—a basic something of the Grecian influence upon the Roman world, I'm sent on my way very like a tradesman. I roil with frustration, but so begins my voyage of incarnation and destruction; inception and death; prelude and coda. I'm Odysseus reborn.

The mere retelling leaves me exhilarated! I reach for brushes and oils.

OLD GREY.

Today I favour Old Grey. My method for its preparation is as follows: burn up a quantity of fresh peach-stones within a closed vessel. Cherrystones will likewise serve, but never so well. Take up a heavy granite mortar and pestle to crush them into obedience. Once the mixture's rendered fine add an equal amount of White Lead, likewise a good quantity of proper oil, then grind away conscientiously until a smooth paste forms.

The twenty-first day of January
in the year of Our Lord 1775.

Today's the day set aside to laud Saint Agnes of Rome, the virgin martyr. It's said that anyone attempting her rape would be promptly struck blind. That, or worse: in response to her fervent prayers God would smother her body from head to toe in thick hair, thus presenting a formidable deterrent to male attentions of the dishonourable kind.

Cavaliere,

What provokes a man to undertake the tortures of travel? Do you ever wonder? Look beyond the inconvenience: voyaging expands the mind, spurring it into activity, and an active mind will amplify the experiences to come. England's too small a stage for me, but before I drink down the delights of your homeland, Cavaliere, there's work to be done here in London. It demands my full attention as my esteemed sponsor Milord Halebroke requires much of me. The primary inspiration for my Work must indeed be sucked from breast of heady antiquity, but where to begin? No, no: not there: I'm off to the madhouse of St. Luke's, of course! Perversity, you may think, but where else might I excavate such a rich vein of human *matériel* and nigh on *gratis* to boot?

    The Keepers of St. Luke's will allow entry to the building in return for a small consideration, but my heavier coin grants me closer access. I'm a frequent visitor and they know the depth of my purse. In that asylum, that dismal shrine to lunacy, that mausoleum of madness, I'll seek out a subject blessed with the appropriate physique.

And what a specimen I find! He's newly arrived, but for the sake of propriety I won't reveal his family name, despite his nearest and dearest being the very individuals who had the dear confined him to bedlam in the first place! So, I'll refer to him as "Lord Q". In his family's defence, however, Lord Q's a violent lunatic and prone to outbursts of the most perplexing, frightening kind. This may explain the heavy chains fixing him to the wall.

Permit me to relate the specifics of his initial confinement. Come his last evening of freedom his ever-loving family decide in close conference that they can no longer endure his angry flailing about and sundry other unmentionable tendencies, so a Keeper from St. Luke's is quickly summoned.

Upon arrival the man's first question is how he might identify his patient, being anxious to pin him down and dress him up, with alacrity, in his "special waist-coat". All this must be accomplished with as little fuss as possible and with no danger to patient, witness and, most importantly, the Keeper himself.

'He ... is ... in ... there,' instructs a histrionic Lady Q, employing the most absurd stage whisper, 'and he's wearing his second-best brown coat. Above all that you'll recognise him straight away on account of his raving. Oh, and I should also warn you that he's ably strong in the body and inclined to resist.'

At this news our Keeper, already strung up on tenterhooks, being understandably fearful of injury to his person, grows warier still. But then, in a rare moment of courage—yet all the while demonstrating a fondness for the melodramatic—he glides furtively into the room, all stealth and grim intent, the straight-jacket concealed behind his back and both eyes fixed doggedly on the inhabitant of the chair facing away from him. But then calamity: it's not the madman but our Constable, likewise brown coated, who sits with his back to the door! Confusion reigns!

Now then, Lord Q has a prime view of the Keeper's entrance and, in that quick, cunning way many lunatics have he controls his ravings in an instant, scenting a heaven-sent opportunity for more mischief. Our Constable, however, continues to remonstrate with Lord Q and, being a passionate man, flail his arms in the air. Can you guess what pretty piece of theatre ensues? Lord Q catches the Keeper's eye, offers him a conspiratorial wink and nods significantly in the direction of our unsuspecting Constable. The sweating, but expert Keeper has the confounded Officer of the Court gagged and jacketed in a thrice. It's twenty minutes—and more!—before he can be persuaded of his error and by this time Lord Q's made his escape up onto the roof. There, among the gargoyles, balanced upon a parapet, he divests himself of that obfuscating brown coat, followed swiftly by all his other garments, and sets on to bark and howl at the moon. Whenever his bladder allows he also delights himself in trying his best to piss over the watchers gathered below.

I grow rather fond of Lord Q. He sits commendably still for me, aided by his being so robustly fixed to the wall. I sketch out his form in charcoal—muscles, bone-shapes, hair, shadows—and all the while he engages me in pretty and unusual conversation. He's an admirably learned man: a product of Oswestry School and St. John's Cambridge, no less. And witty to boot! He sums up the circumstances of his committal as follows:

'Damn it, Sir Artist!' says he, 'They claimed I was ... umm ... mad! To my very face! I declared them mad, cracked, for daring to suggest such a thing, but this only made them all ... umm ... more choleric still! Damnation: they outvoted me! So that was that and ... umm ... here I am! Petty vengeance, the skulking cowards! They had their hands on my money before I was out of the door. Now then! I will sit for you and ... umm ... await my banishment.'

Banishment? If from here, then to where? Where has this poor soul left to go? A pause ensues while I ponder, but then he asks me this:

'Sir Artist: will you ... umm ... allow me to draw you ... umm ... once my own portrait's done?'

I agree, and with alacrity for the sake of the amusement. I only hope his efforts will prove less than mine, or I'll be forced to adopt his work and proclaim it a self-portrait. There, in that sad, benighted place, I take up a charcoal and draw a handsome man at the end of life and reason, at the very moment of his final descent into lunacy. Is this zenith or nadir? I apply charcoal to paper, combing out and cleaning his lank, prematurely greying hair and calming his agitated features. I transform Lord Q into my bold Heracles. How he laughs at that. Then we laugh together, long and low, at another thought: my patron, while knowing nothing at all of what I'm presently about, is paying me—and most handsomely—to render images of a dispossessed, crazed lunatic to adorn the walls of his precious Long-room. What piquant comedy! Divine.

But his demands don't stop there; Lord Q has stipulations:

'I would have ... umm ... my hair prepared ... umm ... more thus!'

He runs his hands here and there through his locks with alarming results. I attempt a diversion:

'I care little for fopperies.'

'I know, I know, but if I'm to be ... umm ... represented, then surely I must be represented honestly?'

I humour him and the inmate-barber comes, coarse-skilled, shake-handed from gin, but enough to satisfy Lord Q. My subject's wonderfully enthused. I learn a thing of significance that had entirely passed me by: he must be kept content if the experiment's to succeed.

When the barber's done I can perceive little positive good effect, but nevertheless tell Lord Q how fine he looks. More advice for you, Cavaliere: always rebut sound evidence in the cause of an advantageous lie, even when the fact's a ton weight and its repudiation a feather. Progress is the thing, no matter the path, and survival's the *causa causans* of everything. Everything! But heed this well: prepare your lies with the greatest care;

they'll dictate what ensues, pontificating, directing you unto death.

Something more occurs to me: what do you know of the madhouse, Cavaliere? You should acquaint yourself, as should we all. Our existence is so very brittle. Every one of us runs the risk of arriving at such a pretty pass should our world tilt even a little. Any one of us may wake up one day to find himself utterly lost in a foreign place, at the far corner of the map, or hidden in the dusty crease. This knowledge alone should be enough to injure the mind. We may, much like Lord Q., have the simple misfortune to fall foul of a jealous relative who's cast a covetous eye in the direction of our fame or fortune.

That said, bedlams are quite the most exciting of places: all points of the human compass, every caste, every hue of our creature-colour are there to be found. Every dimension of character, age and experience co-exist, but jumbled up; a veritable feast for the observant.

Herewith a sop to the English: *"define true madness / What is't but to be nothing else but mad"*, asks Polonius.

But don't we all grow just a little cracked given enough time? Or become a touch mercurial in the face of life's constant depredations? Have you never felt your senses unravel, even a little? Can you honestly assure me that no insane thought has ever bemused or frightened you? Perhaps prodded you into some reckless hornet's nest of action? Have you never dreamed? Never entertained a single insane notion? Never? I doubt that very much.

The ship of madness sails close-hauled into the wind of Reason; very close indeed; direct into the teeth of the gale, in fact. In the midst of life's silly muddle, mired in human confusion, I wonder if it's my bedlamites, picking doggedly away at their private tangle, who'll one day unravel the world's confusion; uncover that mysterious pattern that eludes the rest of us. "Eureka!" they'll shout to a fly on the wall and wait impatiently for a reply.

We live in the Dark Age of Reason, you see, or if you prefer, in the bright light of *un*reason. I'm no longer certain on which horizon the sun will rise tomorrow: over here, or over there in the company of our febrile Lord Q.

There's a third member of the nobility in my story. Does the Lord of Misrule feature in your folklore, Cavaliere? In St. Luke's they allow him to patrol the halls, will-o'-the-wisp, and have him sit in judgement on any controversy, large or small. He governs passably well. At least his people think so and perhaps that's all that really matters. Today, there are more than three thousand such unfortunates locked away in the asylums dotted here and there across our little island. They live, close-confined, in a murky underworld, swelling in numbers by the day as if, one by one, those of us left in Reason's unforgiving grip are renouncing this existence to run, helter-skelter, in search of a little comfort elsewhere. When *alma mater* fails, *alma anywhere* is a profound temptation.

St Luke's is a veritable *Circus Maximus*. For a single penny bold gentlemen and their nervous ladies may enter the place to study the mad, gawp at the furiously mad and steal an anxious peek at the deafening, menacing quietness of the utterly lost. All this, they doubtless protest, is for their own edification, but I believe their real aim is simple amusement. Where else might they be encouraged to so freely gloat at those less fortunate than themselves? To St. Luke's they come to witness the squalor, gasp at the noise, start at the sudden violence of lives driven by baseness and purest barbarity. Those who are in it, embrace it, while those without applaud the spectacle as if watching seals at play in a penny circus. There it is, Cavaliere: the savage heart of the human soul in all its dread finery: both watcher and watched in curious symmetry.

Charcoal and paper are put away and my newfound Heracles sealed up in my sketchbook. He's no docile prisoner, beating impatiently at the covers and clamouring for release.

    I pack up my necessaries and have them sent ahead of me to Rome. Within a week I'll follow them, setting out with the generous Milord Halebrokes's letter of credit warm in my pocketbook, a heavy purse of his coin in hand for incidentals and, ready formed in mind, a truly excellent plan. I twist and chink the Guinea-coins, savouring their weight as I ponder the Work to come. It will be beautiful and rendered more handsome still by the piquancy that Rome will lend the admixture. The city's fecund with noise, tension and controversy: visceral and deliciously fell. It's been this way since the Etruscans, sucking up its life force from deep pagan roots.

I'll be able to afford the choicest of accommodations, but instead will find my place among the humblest of quarters. This is my *modus operandi*. Perverse, you might well think, but I do all this for excellent reasons. Once in Rome I'll take rooms a hop-step from the stews. Such places spread, cancer-like, through any place the lower social strata congeal; human detritus; infection; stink; painful want. In truth I prefer the inhabitants of St. Luke's, but needs must.

I'll pay in advance. The *genus* of the place will welcome me. Here's a place of brooding menace in which my incipient scheme might flourish; a butterfly emerging from its chrysalis. Anyway, the more prosperous parts of the city are awash with many too many of my "fellow artists". In truth they're little better than slack-jawed tourists intent on drinking down as much of the city's artistic liturgy as they can within the bare week or two they've allowed for this slice of their "Grand Tour". I'll assiduously avoid their company. They're braying donkeys to a man; braggarts one and all; facile, visionless amateurs.

My humble lodgings will prove perfect and my landlord discrete. My window will overlook a little *piazza*, a fountain bubbling away in the centre. There, the whole world will lie in view. The hubbub will keep my loneliness at bay. My landlord will leave me to myself and the food will be fresh, simple and nourishing; the wine an inspiration.

I'll set to work at once, a quantity of Burnt Umber ready to hand.

BURNT UMBER.

My favoured method for the preparation of Burnt Umber is this: obtain an adequate quantity of the brown clay pigment wherein good quantities of iron and manganese are found. Apply heat and observe the essence of Burnt Umber slowly emerge. Be patient. When fully dried out, grind the mixture into a fine powder. Add a generous measure of your best oil. Burnt Umber derives its name from the Latin word "umbra", meaning "shadow", having been first extracted in Umbria, a mountainous region in the centre of the peninsula. It can also be discovered in other parts of the world, but I favour that from Cyprus.

The fifteenth day of August
in the year of Our Lord 1775.

Today's the feast day of Saint Stephen the first King of Hungary. He urged his son Emeric to "be chaste, so that you may avoid all the foulness that so resembles the pangs of death". Hoh, hum ... What hypocrisy! In doing so he denied his son the pleasures he'd himself repeatedly and conspicuously enjoyed; Stephen was a most saintly dissembler.

Cavaliere,

The Work progresses; I bestride the world, but will be gracious in victory as befits a gentleman. That said, I urge you to remember that both my success and your failure were assured from the beginning, Genesis to Revelation, so don't blame yourself: the result of our contest was always a foregone conclusion. I'm adept in many things and not least this; the laurels were always bound to fall to me.

I observe you from afar as you hold court, attended by sycophants and minions. One day I come so close as to perceive the greying hair at your ears and the creasing skin around your eyes. Blame me for that. Meeting me is enough to raise the heartbeat; challenging me is sufficient to make life stutter. Do you understand nothing of what you've taken on? I am blight; I am locust; I am the sudden death of trust.

Those in my circle who once thought well of me have been all-too easily misled. My loyal, trusting friends stopped up their ears in my cause. Had they gulped down the soup of scurrilous rumour, laced with innuendo, garnished with a little accusation, their consciences might trouble them a little less today. As for you, Cavaliere, know this: there's worse to come. If anything, the accounts of my depravities are conservative: I'm no gradual phenomenon: no white-tending-to-grey, but utterly black; there's nothing betwixt and between. I'm unredeemed, unenlightened and utterly lost.

I know I have champions; loyal friends ready to rise up in my defence and stand by me. To them I say only this: shed tears at your own stupidity. I'm the end of innocence; reason too. There! It's done: my confession complete; conscience appeased.

As to the rightful place of the Artist in life know this: he must rise above common circumstance, or exist forever in shadow. Your lesson-to-come will radiate light onto your place in the continuum of existence, Cavaliere -bureaucrat. It's simple enough: the Artist places a frame around life's canvas to illustrate the things that your kind, Cavaliere, imagine in isolation, but can never assemble into a single composition. For you, Cavaliere, without the Artist's intervention the universe lacks vital coherence. I am vision and perspective. In my right hand I hold my brush, in my left my pallet. Before me stands a wide, empty canvas: an acre of revelation-to-come. I undertake this sacred Labour in the service of humanity, Cavaliere. I'm your private blessing. One day you'll give thanks to have known me. I'll be raised up.

My sense of triumph is short lived: the very next day I find myself ill and altogether gloomy. My skin's become a little like parchment to the touch.

But let's establish a vital boundary: I must be found guilty (*in absentia*) of the sins for which I'm responsible and no more. My deeds are certain to provoke imitation from weak-minded individuals; charlatans to a man; incapable of original thought and not one of them worthy to be my lowliest student.

Know also this: I'll not allow any of my triumphs to be attributed to another hand. My distinction's upon them all, so their provenance cannot be doubted. Within my oeuvre you'll detect a continuum: coherence and cohesion.

Oh, and I also take note of the darkened flesh around your eyes, Cavaliere. Anyone might think you plagued by sleeplessness from worry, or some mysterious malady. I beg you to consult a reputable physician: you have a long road to travel. Are you strong enough? Your own contribution to the Work is this: to ensure that every one of my sins is properly ascribed to me; they are my Art, and mine alone; I'll brook no pretenders.

And so to business.

The First Labour of Heracles:
the Nemean Lion.

I arrive in the eternal city. I come by ship—most uncomfortably—into Pisa and continue by carriage, less comfortably—along the Via Aurelia. At one point I resort to bumping along on horseback. I dislike ships, but find riding still worse. I'm awkward in the saddle and doubtless unbecoming to look at. I hear that you're fond of riding, Cavaliere, ergo you must be fond of the consequent sweating, chaffing thighs and sore arse.

Heracles' first act of penance for his crime was to slay the Nemean Lion. Born of the Chimera, the beast terrorised the people the length and breadth of Nemea in the valley of the River Elissos. The Lion was vicious; formidable, with a hide so thick no arrow or lance could penetrate. So what could our hero do? At last, on the very edge of despair Heracles wrestled the beast to ground, thrust his arm down its throat and choked it to death. He flensed the corpse and carried his gory trophy back to King Eurystheus to prove his first Labour complete.

So where to find my Nemean Lion? He must roar furiously at the world and shake his mane at the gods. I require posture, bombast and militancy in my subject. He'll be combative. Deadly.

I strive in vain until one day my Lion comes to me demanding, most imperiously, that I depict him in the full dress uniform of his rank. Tenente Colonello Cesare Guastalla is the epitome of martial perfection. Formerly of the Sardinia-Piedmont army he's lately transformed himself into a faithful servant of the Papal States, the cunning fellow. He's a veteran of sundry violent battles and is impressively scarred in face and limb. Here's a man to be taken seriously. Before me stands my Lion. He lives quietly and is, therefore, also a most convenient Lion.

I confess this first chapter of the Work to be almost pleasurable: Tenente Colonello Guastalla's quite charming and has experienced much in life. We talk. From his lips I learn that you, Cavaliere di Credico, have pursued me to these shores, returning first to Fiorenze with your daughter and then forging onward, alone, to Rome.

Your daughter? There's happy news indeed and more to follow; my intelligencers rarely disappoint. She's a great beauty, or so says the Tenente Colonello. She's to live at your home in Florence while you, Cavaliere, conduct your business here in Rome. I understand the true nature of this "business" very well, but my Lion-soldier doesn't realise that you have, in fact, returned to Rome in pursuit of me! I also discover the name of this beauteous creature: Sophia. *Sophia Amelia di Credico*. Such wonderful poesy! A name to be conjured with; an evocation of ... something ... yes: a pulse beating beneath pale, noble skin; untarnished by the sun and unscarred by manual work. *Sophia*.

This morning Kabalos instructs me to prepare quantities of the dominant colour for the piece in hand.

MILORI BLUE.

An "Iron Blue", "Milori Blue", "Bronze Blue", "Steel Blue", or as it is styled by the Germans, "Parisian Blue", draws its strength—its power— from a blue-green mineral. The colour will fade a little if mixed with white, but used in isolation I find it strong and permanent. Its drying time's unexceptional, but it will give a hard-yet-flexible finish. But be sure not to breathe in the dust: even a robust man such as you, Cavaliere, *is unlikely to survive that. We live in such dangerous times.*

In the midst of my preparations I recall my parents, but I know not why. What a sad inspiration they were. *Mutter* und *Vater* would have preferred me to build myself a dull little cottage out of mud and thatch, while I'd set my heart on pyramids, ornate temples and pleasure-domes. Could they have even imagined me here in Rome? I doubt it.

On we go. Kabalos keeps himself close at hand, concealed from sight behind a screen and muttering instructions, *sotto voce*, to me as I work. He sows wild thoughts into my mind.

We make good progress until one day I change our arrangement:

'Colonello!' say I, as I surprise him in the street outside his home: 'I beg a moment of your time.'

'Whatever you require, Signore Beade. Anything!'

'A pressing family matter calls me home.'

'Ah, but what then of my portrait?'

Note that he displays no concern for my "pressing family matter". Such self-centredness!

'It's barely half done, I know, so I've come to plead with you. I can finish the canvas without delay, but ask only that you sit late into the night for me. Perhaps tomorrow? Would that be suitable?'

He grumbles, of course, but nevertheless comes to my rooms the following evening as arranged. I hope—no, indeed I pray—that no one else is aware of our assignation. I take no foolhardy risks, but then, without piquancy, the game will become pure tedium. Come evening we share a meal, his portion infused with a measure of Paracelsus' ingredients, but this time most carefully formulated. My calculations must be accurate this time; here's no Mary, but a Nemean Lion!

I set to work by the candlelight, the Roman skyline burning red in the dying of the day. I fear he may wake to my purpose too soon and wage war on me, but in the end all goes well. After a little time, while yet conscious the Tenente Colonello loses the ability to manipulate his limbs. Soon enough his speech follows suit and thereafter it's a simple matter until the end. I stifle his breath, but employ a ligature of fine silk as befits his station in life; a simple kindness to a friend.

The unfinished portrait's immediately consigned to the flames; such damning evidence must never be discovered. In any case, it's a dull, pedestrian thing displaying little of my usual flair. A fresh canvas awaits. Heracles flensed his lion, as do I, revealing the Tenente

Colonello's musculature to my close inspection. An Artist must study at his Art, as I've said. Although I'm less expert with knife than brush I afford him every possible courtesy. I have my lion's hide rolled-up hide beside me as I write, Cavaliere: a worthy *memento mori*. It will find its way to you in good time. His family may wish to reunite hide with bones, but I leave this to you.

Then I play the Five-Point Game; a simple concept, but demanding much of the Artist. Here's how to play: place five points at random upon a blank canvas and then contrive some way of portraying a human subject with each of the extremities—two feet, two hands and the top of the head—touching one of the five marks.

I've added another facet to the game; my singularity, distinction; a private *frisson* unique to me. Here it is: the canvas must be finished within a single night, before the last of a hundred candles gutters and dies.

I work by their wavering light until dawn comes and the Work's complete. In truth it's a wonderful: remarkable to behold. I've grafted the much-refined visage of our lunatic Lord Q, pictured in his prime, onto the broad shoulders of my fine-bodied classical warrior.

Lord Q would be greatly entertained to see how my Heracles, rendered in the classical style, stands over the doomed lion, spear raised, ready to strike the beast down. What violence! What majesty! The lion fights to the last, maw agape and talons bared, a trial of ferocity and brute strength.

Milord Halebroke will be pleased; delighted, I'm sure, if he can grasp the cleverness of its execution. But there, below the lion in the corner of the canvas, hidden in the shadows, is a privy message for you, Cavaliere di Credico: a wild, seven-headed Hydra. It's small, lurking there in the gloom, but sufficient to hint at my next victim. Will you detect it? Then will you have the wit to understand what you see? I can't be sure. Will you smoke my intent? Unlikely; I'm throwing bones to a toothless dog. In any case, it's much too early in my strategy for you to draw the vital connection; every sword must be sharpened, armour made ready and spear-blade honed.

As arranged, come dawn two nameless, faceless men arrive to dispose of an equally nameless, faceless corpse. As far as their world is concerned I've completed my anatomisation and recording the musculature of an executed man's cadaver. There's no possibility of the body being recognised, of course, with it lacking a face. What's left of the Tenente Colonello's body will most likely grace the table of an enthusiastic student of medicine, knife in hand, ambition burning in his eye. Tenente Colonello Cesare Guastalla has been erased from the world. I'll miss him a little, the dear.

Nota Bene—I've found my first grey hairs, there at my temples. I thought myself too young for this and am saddened.

**The nineteenth day of September
in the year of Our Lord 1775.**

*On this, the feast day of Saint Januarius of Kolb
patron saint of volcanoes, visitors attending the
splendid cathedral in Naples may witness the
miraculous liquefaction of blood on his statue.*

Hoh, hum.

The Second Labour of Heracles:
the Lernæan Hydra.

Heracles' second endeavour was to dispatch the Lernæan Hydra: a swamp-dwelling, many-headed atrocity teased from the depths of the Underworld and able to kill with breath alone. I've encountered a few of that creature's Overworld acolytes: ill mannered, uncouth and foul-mouthed to a man and woman. Low conversation appals me and on several occasions I've found myself reaching for the dagger I keep about me when out of doors. Society would be a sweeter thing with fewer such vulgar braggarts lurking in dark corners.

To business: the Hydra has more heads than can be painted on a Greek vase and, of course, that deathly poisonous breath. The execution of the preliminary sketch takes some time and before I can start work on the canvas-proper I receive a visitation from none other than yourself, Cavaliere.

'Signore Beade,' you say, head dipping your head slightly to the left. I'm sure I can see yet more flecks of grey hair in the midst of your coiffure. Are we walking the same path?

You adopt a confidential tone and that familiar, calculated half-smile. I observe you silently and impassively for a long moment. Flustered at my silence you speak again: 'I learned of your presence here in Rome and could not resist renewing our acquaintance. It is a joy to meet you again.'

Cavaliere, think I, you're a fraud and a charlatan. I find no joy in your presence, nor you in mine, and all this is no coincidence. Your family home's in Florence and if you had any sense at all you would be there, enjoying the company of your daughter while you still can.

'And here you are hard at work! Might I be allowed to see the piece?'

'It's unfinished, but ...'

I reveal *Heracles Slaying the Nemean Lion* and begin to explain my various conjurings with colour.

'Wondrous. It is, well ... such a clever use of light and shade.'

The absence of *points d'exclamation* is no oversight on my part; you're emotionless, and no connoisseur of fine art. Cavaliere, you're entirely ignorant of its delicate and complex workings. You thrash about, here and there, searching for something vaguely flattering to say.

PIGMENT OF GOLD.

Lightened with white from calcined hartshorn—eschewing white lead, this being the ingredient most commonly recommended—and combined with an Arsenic Yellow: "Yellow Orpiment", which is also "King's Yellow" or "Chinese Yellow", and "Red Orpiment", occasionally termed "Realgar" or "Risalgallo", this will produce a most useful oil. But never touch it with an iron knife, Cavaliere, and certainly never taste it! It's deathly poisonous. I must also mention that without my secret improvements Orpiments are impermanent.

I politely repost one lackwit question after another, but inwardly I seethe: in no way are you qualified to sit in judgement on my Work, nor indeed that of any reputable Artist, yet on the outside I present myself as a paradigm of patience while you plough on:

'It owes much to the modern style. I see that. Some elements appear to have been rendered in haste, but I expect you have more to do before the world sees it.'

Modern style? Never in life! Words for their own sake, but at least your dredging about reveals something of you.

'It's unfinished, as you say. As I've said it's a work in progress, Cavaliere; a preliminary canvas only. See here: another sketch-work yet to be rendered in oil.'

'Ah! I see! Here ...'

You extend an enquiring finger. The Hydra! You detect the Hydra at first glance. Have I underestimated you?

'And what is this I see here? Is this the Lernæan Hydra? It is! Of course! There is Hercules' second Labour. How ingenious of you to allude to the next in the sequence.'

"Hercules". There it is again. And yet I'm both surprised and impressed at such an uncharacteristic, though flawed, display of learning.

'I thank you again. Are you familiar with the *Heraclean* Labours, Cavaliere?'

You hesitate, detecting the admonition.

'A little.'

'Then I encourage you to study them further and in close detail. So much of life lies there, ready to be discovered, Cavaliere.'

'You are doubtless correct, Signore Beade, but now I must be on my way and ... oh, I also seek news of a man known to you.'

'Indeed?'

'The Tenente Colonello Cesare Guastalla. An officer belonging to a regiment quartered close to the city.'

'I know the man. What of him?'

'He has disappeared. Utterly disappeared.'

That familiar long, silent look arrows in my direction once again. I respond with silence. You take your leave, frustration writ large, suspicion piled up on suspicion. I'm relieved and troubled both at once. You'll never match my intellect, that's clear, but I begin to see the tenacity and determination that so recommends you to your Austrian masters.

Onward we go: the nine-headed Hydra, child of Typhon and Echidna, dwelt in a foul-smelling swamp beside the Lake of Lerna in the Argolid. Nine heads, eight mortal, one immortal. Lerna's the portal to the Underworld at which the Hydra stood sentinel, barring access to man and beast. A cloth tied over nose and mouth against the fumes and shooting flaming arrows into the depths of its lair, Heracles forced the thing out into the light and confronted it in arms. Battle duly commenced, but each time Heracles hacked off one poison-spewing head with his harvesting sickle—why that, of all things? —two grew back in its place!

Despairing, our hero called upon his *eromenos*, his nephew Iolaus, to aid him in the fight. Inspired, the lad suggested that they cauterize each stump with a flaming brand the moment a head was severed. Such efficiency! Such industry! Finally, the last—and the immortal—head was hacked off and buried under great rock beside the sacred way between Lerna and Elaius. Heracles, one eye on the future, dipped his arrows in the Hydra's blood to make them lethally poisonous. Clever fellow! Take note, Cavaliere: he, like me, planned ahead.

So whom will I find to play the part of my Hydra? Kabalos is ready with an answer. On the banks of the Tiber lies a veritable swamp of sin and destitution. Here, the army of brothel madams is impossible to conquer: as soon as one's imprisoned another springs up, Hydra-like, in her place. I venture forth and have her picked out in an instant.

'Signora.'

'Signor<u>ina</u>.'

'Of course. My apologies. I'm a man of ... err ... considerable appetites, but today I've only a little money about me ...'

Her expression sours in the blink of an eye; rejection looms.

'So allow me to put a business proposition to you.'

A look of intrigue elbows suspicion aside.

'Father Time marches relentlessly on, even for a rare beauty such as you, Signorina! I assume you've already had someone capture your image while yet in its prime. No? Then hear me now! I simply must paint you, and in your finest gown. In return I ask only for an agreed amount of credit, and that to be redeemed in your establishment alone. Better still, only when you've witnessed the quality of my Work will I ask you to determine the amount of credit I am to enjoy. However, our arrangement must be a close-kept secret; I have my reputation to consider. Discretion, you understand?'

She thinks, but not overlong: vanity's a god to us all and demands regular sacrifice. I begin her portrait the same night. Kabalos is emboldened, but keeps himself invisible until the last moment. We take off her head at midnight and bury it under a rock beside the Via Appia. Her body we consign to the Tiber.

My brushstrokes are deft, efficient, and the next canvas assumes form and proportion in short order. Hidden within it's your next clue, Cavaliere: in the upper right quartile of *Heracles Slaying the Lernæan Hydra* a magnificent golden stag flees toward the safety of the trees. But then I detect a slight tremor in my right hand. I pray that it will cease and not return before the Work's complete.

YELLOW ORPIMENT.

I observed a fly crawl into a small amount of Yellow Orpiment and perish after a series of dramatic spasms. Orpiment, much admired for its brilliant yellow pigment, is sometimes known as "King's Yellow", or "Chinese Yellow". It's also a most effective poison.

**The seventeenth day of October
in the year of Our Lord 1775.**

Today's the feast day of Saint Ignatius of Antioch, who was famously devoured by lions in the Colosseo. In death he at least discovered how to be a little useful.

Your agents observe me day and night, Cavaliere di Credico, but they're ham fisted and incompetent to a man. They fail miserably to blend into the crowd as they stalk me along street and alleyway. They don't reckon on my keen Artist's eye. I'm not discouraged one iota from the business in hand, but their presence provokes me, Cavaliere; you should have the courage to confront me in person. I'm growing very, very angry with you. I see what you have in mind. Were you to speak up, you might say:

'I know very well what you are about, Signore Beade. Make the slightest mistake and I will have a noose tight around your neck before dusk.'

The game's truly begun.

The Third Labour of Heracles:
the Golden Stag.

The Golden Stag, an androgynous Ceryneian Hind, was sacred to chaste Artemis, goddess of the hunt and protector of female virginity. The gold-antlered and bronze-hoofed beast was so fleet of foot it could outrun an arrow in flight. A truly formidable opponent.

King Eurystheus, furious that Heracles had thus far cheated death and yet too cowardly to challenge him in person, planned his third penance with great cleverness. He hoped that Heracles' crime would so anger Artemis that she'd punish him severely. Ordered Heracles to capture the stag unharmed, our hero obediently pursued the luckless creature for an entire year, running the length and breadth of Greece until the beast finally lay down, utterly spent, unable to run another step.

Hero and quarry returned to Eurystheus who, while disappointed at Heracles' success, was nonetheless delighted at the prospect of adding such a marvellous prize to his menagerie. He ventured forth from his palace to take possession of his gift, but the moment Heracles released it into his hands the fabled Ceryneian Hind broke free and fled back to Artemis' fond embrace. How our hero must have laughed at that! And how Eurystheus must have scowled!

Now who to cast in the role of the Golden Stag? Kabalos gives the matter great consideration. Much exaggerated pondering ensues. Crouched in a corner, his outsized, misshapen head cradled in hand, he waits patiently until a wave of inspiration breaks across him at last: my quarry will be Alfredo Scipione, the effeminate Venetian actor currently enjoying great fame in Rome. You showered him with fawning approbation, Cavaliere, as I observed you from a private box in the theatre, directly opposite your own, as Scipione performed Metastasio's *Ruggiero*. I saw you clap your hands together in the manner of a circus seal. You leant forward in your enthusiasm, a ridiculous smile wreathing your face. You utter booby! All this for such a low piece of stagecraft, much of it borrowed from Ariosto, and Metastasio's meagre contribution was emphatically dull.

Scipione was an easy man to court, his strutting vanity plain for all to see. There will be a great many in the city delighted to see him brought low.

I bend his vanity against him like this:

'Signore Scipione! I admire your work immensely.'

'Indeed, Signore ...'

'Beade. Aloysius Amerigo Beade, at your service.'

'The painter?'

'Artist. I'm no decorator, Signore. You're familiar with my work?'

'Of course! You painted that dolt Abbiati, no?'

'I regret I cannot claim that distinction, but I have served others. Your friend Signore Gandolfo, for example.'

'Hah! Gandolfo. I saw it: a flattering portrait of an incorrigible fool! On stage he usually has the look of a man enduring a particularly painful shit!'

He cackles triumphantly, looks about him and soaks up the approval of his simpering acolytes. He offers a bow and I reciprocate graciously before saying:

'But who will have the honour of painting of you, Signore?'

'Me?'

A false modesty: the question's already on his mind.

'How can you allow Gandolfo to grace someone's wall for eternity while your own, infinitely more deserving public, are prevented from gazing upon your image and recalling your wonderful achievements? And you the more accomplished performer by a country mile!'

'You're too kind. Perhaps ...'

'I would be greatly honoured, Signore, to render such a service.'

It was as easy as that, the buffoon! But before I could begin this chapter of the Work I was to have the pleasure of your company once again, Cavaliere, and this time your mood bordered on the hostile:

'I know very well it was you, Signore Beade. I am certain of it. The Hydra in your painting was pointing to the subject of your next canvas. A procuress! I should have guessed. And here, in the next painting, another clue lies hidden. It must be here somewhere, but where to find it in such a tangle of images? Such confusion! What do you intend for me to pick out? How am I to interpret this? Is this it? Or perhaps it is the moon, there? But who, or what might the moon represent? Or is it this animal, *here*? What does this portray? A pig, perhaps? No, not that. That's impossible. A strange looking beast, in any case; badly worked, I might say. And this thing is simply foolish, is it not? Most unrealistic. No? Or is this the clue? Perhaps not.'

You're confounded, then certain. Confused again, then accusing, by turns. Do I see uncertainty growing in your mind like a weed? What's more, you find yourself utterly powerless: being no *aficionado* of art. The task unmans you; you're an unlettered schoolboy facing a test. There's your Achilles Heel; there it is.

I must admit that Signore Scipione depicted in the form of a golden stag evolves into a thing of rare beauty. His immortal representation's a considerable improvement on his mortal form. But did you detect the inaccuracy? In Heracles' third trial the stag lives, but I have much more to do and the dead can accuse no one.

The month of May brings the Festival of the Ascension. On the outskirts of the city is a commonplace barn in which stands a crucified Jesus carved out of wood.

It's a monstrous, gaudy thing intended to be carried shoulder-high through the Roman streets to celebrate our murdered Lord's crucifixion. More wondrous still, every inch of the thing's plastered in lustrous gold leaf intended to radiate the morning light and dazzle the gawping onlookers. Imagine his astonishment when the sculptor arrives the next morning, flask and bread in hand, with only a day's work in mind, to discover his tribute's been made a touch more life-like: trickling from wounds around its head, hands and feet and from the gaping wound in its side is real blood. A miracle? No: perfectly mundane; both blood and wounds are only too real. Here's something decidedly worldly: murder. This, Cavaliere, is Signore Scipione's final, and by far his worthiest performance.

The next message lies concealed in my next canvas. For your eyes only, Cavaliere: a boar attacks the hind in concert with Heracles, driving its tusks into the animal's soft underbelly. You'll find no such a thing in any account of the Labours, but I'm exercising an Artist's prerogative: life, like literature, is necessarily incomplete. In your quest for the sublime, in your quest for ultimate truth, look no further than Art.

MINIUM.

To create a workable Minium place a quantity of red lead into a well-heated litharge and boil for several hours over a charcoal fire. Observe the pigment emerge, ranging from orange to a brilliant scarlet red. Extract the salt with the aid of distilled vinegar and the remainder will not fade. But beware of its tendency to brush out poorly. It's also a heavy, earthy and decidedly poisonous powder.

The twelfth day of November in the year of Our Lord 1775.

Today's the feast day of Saint Josaphat Kuntsevych. He's every inch a saint in the eyes of il Vaticano, but to this day Kuntsevych is furiously loathed by his countrymen. A brutal tyrant, he was set upon and murdered by a mob of the very people he sought to oppress. A prophet's rarely welcomed in his home town.

The Fourth Labour of Heracles:
the Erymanthian Boar.

Stephen, my own dear Iolaus, my constant armiger, my *eromenos*, is come to me at last. He's here in Rome! I'm much heartened, having become lonely. His presence warms me. It's said that we're strangely alike and that I could easily pass for Stephen and he for me. I'll make good use of this; you'll see how. How shall I describe him? The strong line of his jaw? Or perhaps the gentlemanly set of his hair? He has several teeth set crooked and a bad way of blinking when he speaks a lie, but all that said he has my confidence.

I didn't send for him: he divined my needs by instinct and came to find me. I count him my truest, most loyal friend. He's also an artist of some talent and I'm his tutor in life and art, light and dark. We meet in my rooms to share a flask of good wine. As I serve him my right hand trembles so much that I'm forced to use my left. Stephen takes the flask from me and pours the wine himself.

He reaffirms his solemn vow: to assist me in all things, anything, my Great Undertaking notwithstanding. He speaks the words with touching solemnity. Now that you, the Cavaliere di Credico, have me so closely observed, Stephen will be able to pass through the city streets freely while I lead your buffoons astray and, with us being so similar in appearance—*we might easily be taken for twin brothers*—can also take my place should the need ever arise. Your badger-legged, bed-presser bloodhounds will be forever snuffling after the wrong scent.

His passion for Art is truly wonderful and, like me, he's not overburdened with any of the—*how shall I say this?*—conventional sensibilities; such things are dangerous, they sap the vitality away from we men of moment. Stephen, Kabalos and I, the triumvirate, will now be joined together until the Work's complete. Or are we musicians come together in joyous symphony? Yes! Harmony, the fundamental spirit, surrounds us all three.

The Erymanthian Boar came roaring out of the Arcadian wilderness: fearsome, strong, indomitable. No mere mortal could possibly outrun the beast, but Heracles—*the consummate tactician!*—chose to perform his deed in midwinter, thus slowing the animal down in the deep snow. After a long chase the Boar, exhausted at last, was captured and presented to Eurystheus, but our foolish king, the utter craven, became so alarmed at the animal's ferocity that he ducked down behind a storage *pithos* and begged Heracles to return the beast from whence it came.

Eurystheus was a fool, but the social order must nevertheless be upheld. Hunters may not be painted as fools and the hunted should understand their role in life. This is the proper way of things.

So where to lay my hands on a suitably brutal Erymanthian Boar? *Fortuna: send me a soul to honour thus!* I pray, and my prayer's quickly answered. The prize fighter Giuseppe's life is the envy of many, but his moral compass is located in his cock. Passion, violence and physique are his obsessions; he's a gladiator, a slum bully who makes his living by pummelling opponents near to death, bare-knuckling for prize money and the rapture of doting ladies. All-comers, most commonly young blades, take their chances against him in the vain hope that, if they're still on their feet come the final bell, both purse and plaudits will be theirs. All this to impress some dim-witted paramour and a motley collection of braying, hooting cronies.

In any case, the bravos invariably stagger home toothless, broken-nosed and bloody, while the women they seek to soften instead stare, wide-eyed, at Giuseppe *Victor*! They adore him from head to toe, more often than not allowing their eyes to linger, for an indecently long moment, somewhere in the middle. They'd drink his sweat if they could; Roman womanhood awed in the presence of a victorious *gladiatore*. It was ever thus.

We step into a closed-down carriage and off we go, rattling through the Roman countryside as far as Tivoli. It snows, blessing our venture, muting our noise and keeping the curious behind their doors. Our journey goes all-but unnoticed. Giuseppe swallows down great quantities of a strong, heady wine with Paracelsus' prescription laced liberally into his measure. Stephen's profoundly unlike me in this way: he loathes alcohol, but nonetheless smacks his lips together in appreciation purely for the sake of our little drama. Giuseppe relishes each draught noisily, becoming evermore voluble and, at the same time, crucially pliable.

We arrive for our "hunt" in the gardens of the Villa d'Este. I can most heartily recommend their beauty under a covering of snow, Cavaliere, but even with the spectacular Hundred Fountains Alley for a backdrop the chase proves disappointing. Guiseppe submits far too quickly; he grovels, pleading for his life. How shameful! Our boxer should at least outlast the first few rounds! We do, however, recapture a little of the violence required for the Work as I shoot him square through his chest. For the purposes of the piece Heracles is pictured standing over the dying animal, drawn bow in hand, arrow set to make an end of the mighty beast. Centre left stands a cow, looking on incuriously, in shadow, ruminating; the next clue, of course.

I know you're intercepting my correspondence, Cavaliere, but you'll learn nothing from the letters I receive from my sister, nor will my replies afford you the slightest advantage. I'm altogether too careful for that, but I hope you appreciated the amusing little puzzlements I sowed therein to mystify you; "red herrings", I believe they're called. Did you detect this one?

> *My Dearest Ursula,*
> *I thank-you for your letter and the fine gloves; the Roman artisans are also proficient in leatherwork, but they're nonetheless gratefully received.*
>
> *Should you decide to visit me here, that's if you can be persuaded to leave mother's side for longer than a*

day, I promise you a visit to La Fontana di Trevi. You will delight in the many beautiful reliefs that adorn it: such abundant life, captured in a mountain of cold stone. I find the place fascinating and I spend a deal of time there. The children splash about in the murky water below. Dirty enough to hide ... who knows what? Perhaps we'll see them together one day and uncover a mystery or two.

Et cetera, et cetera, et cetera.

Did you relish a momentary frisson when I dispatched you and your bloodhounds in the direction of Parco Gianicolense? No? Then at what point did you smoke my deception? Or did you guess it from the first? No? Then perhaps you set out, hotfoot, in pursuit of what may be discovered at Colle Palatino. Were you at least a little intrigued? Honestly? You bureaucrats can be so tiresomely dour, lacking imagination and sense of mystery. Incidentally, I've been watching you again: do

I detect a weakness in your step? Is this a new infirmity? Some fresh weakness?

The present Work shows great promise. I envisage a deal of threatening cloud formations set behind and high above.

ROMAN OSTRUM.

My preferred method for the production of a Roman Ostrum of the proper quality, also known as "Tyrian" or "Murex Purple", is simple. Ostrum's also mentioned in antiquity as the "Purple of the Ancients". Ensure you have a sufficient quantity of the correct shellfish to hand and follow the usual procedure. For Pliny, the most desirable shades of Ostrum ranged from reddish/pinkish, to bluish/violet, according to the prevailing fashion. The bluish shade of this colour is occasionally referred to as "Byzantium Purple".

**The seventh day of December
in the year of Our Lord 1775.**

Today's the feast day of Saint Ambrose of Milan. The patron saint of beekeepers, Ambrose was so named after his father witnessed a swarm alight upon the baby's face as he lay in his cradle. In time the bees took wing, leaving the child completely unharmed and a single drop of honey lying on his cheek.

The Fifth Labour of Heracles:
the Augean Stables.

My illness has returned with vehemence: the tremors are much magnified and the white hair at my temples has spread further. Entire days are laid waste while I sweat like a striving horse. Stephen makes progress where he can, but spends too much time attending me. Yet his work does grow in proficiency. He's left-handed, his style very different from mine, but his imitations improve by the day.

I stink. I must stink. Fortunately, my senses—not least my sense of smell—are dulled. Then in the space of a single night my hair turns white and my skin takes on an unpleasant, chalky hue. My Iolaus and I are differentiating, which presents us with a problem: how might he be mistaken for me now? Stephen has a ready solution, colouring his hair to match mine.

What tints might I employ to render a self-portrait of the wreck I see reflected back at me in the looking glass? How to depict my current state with honesty? Few shades of anything bright, that's sure, and nothing strong. Indeed, most of them would be lifeless drab.

I feel so weakened I may as well be dead, but the Work's incomplete and Stephen, although able, is sure to fail if left entirely to his own devices. But there's more convergence: like him I also now favour my left hand over my right, which hangs withered and nigh on paralysed. Progress is slow: I learn ... or rather *un*learn, as I work. The effect's very different from my efforts of even a week past yet not, I think, entirely worse.

I take comfort in one thing alone: I hear reports of an increased tremor in your own limbs, Cavaliere. At first I suspect you're feigning infirmity purely to mock me, but then my reasoning matures: we two must embrace frailty; we're kindred spirits, each one sensing the desperation of the other's loss, but you'll suffer an injury deeper than anything I've ever been dealt. I almost envy you that; plumbing the depths of the human experience is a rare privilege. This is my gift to you.

Heracles fifth Labour went like this: brim-full of the anger roiling in his soul King Eurystheus planned to degrade our hero once again, commanding him to shovel centuries of cowshit from the stables of Augeas King of Elis and all in a single day. Undaunted, Heracles cleverly diverted the rivers Alpheus and Peneus to sweep the accumulated detritus before the flood. Having first promised Heracles the tithe of his fabled herd in return for his success, Augeas reneged on the agreement and an outraged Heracles promptly slaughtered him. Such blind fury was his!

A stable full of animals is beyond the reach of my purse, so a single cow must suffice. But then how to infuse such a pedestrian subject with the necessary sense of majesty?

In the end the inspiration for the fifth canvas comes easily: in my interpretation Heracles strikes the ground with his lance, diverting the rivers to flow through the stables. A flock of birds looks on from above. This last image is entirely for your benefit, Cavaliere.

So to business, but where to find my bovine subject? And then how to induce such a naturally lazy, noisome beast to appear even a tenth part heroic? Revelation comes to me at last: even a milch-mother has a modicum of vanity, or at least a stolid pride in her calling. That must suffice; surely it will. It's at least clever.

I grow wearier still; my time's shortening. On aching feet I conduct my search through the domestic quarter where the moneyed Roman *nobilitas* strut about. I encounter a suitable candidate. Persuaded by a liberating quantity of prime bishop, which he gulps down as I sip primly at my own, the man boasts of his successes and catalogues his many achievements. He even describes his skills as a lover, the braggart, and then how he keeps his fecund wife in a state of semi-permanent gravidity. He insists that she nurture all their offspring at her own breast not only until weaned, but far beyond! No milch-mother for her: she's filling the post admirably well on her own account! He chuckles at his own ingenuity. The Visconte and his exhausted Viscontessa are the proud parents of eight chubby children. My boastful friend speaks of them with glowing pride.

(Nota Bene—Don't be overly impressed with titles: minor nobles are ten-a-penny in these parts and most of them as poor as church-mice.)

He brags so long and loud of his children's musical achievements he would, given the opportunity, festoon the city with jolly bunting in celebration of their many and various scholastic honours. I come to despise the man and, blessed with a merciful nature, decide then and there to liberate their poor, benighted mother from her purgatory.

The Visconte departs the city on business and Stephen seeks out the Viscontessa the very next day:

'Viscontessa,' says he, all fawning respectfulness. 'I beg your leave. I encountered your husband the Visconte only yesterday. When he learned of my Master's great undertaking he insisted that I seek you out. Signore

Beade's an artist ... that's to say a great artist ... engaged by none other than the Holy Father to describe in oil on canvas the various stages in a man's life: from birth to death and then that which awaits us beyond the curtain. Imagine the honour! Commissioned by none other than Saint Peter's heir! But I'm distraught with worry: my Master's sent me out in search of subjects for a particular work—he's a shy man, humble in company; he rarely steps over the threshold of his studio—and I've failed him thus far! I'll be severely punished and justly so! You see, without a representation of *Motherhood's Beauty* the entire series will be incomplete, useless, the whole edifice ruined!

'He's admired you from a distance, Viscontessa, in all propriety, of course, and also your charming children. Beauty—righteous beauty—encircles you, infusing the very air. You must be the subject for *Motherhood's Beauty*: no one else will suffice; nothing less will serve; beauty and motherly compassion radiates from you! You see, he already has a representation of *The Faithful Midwife* on canvas and has more recently completed *God's Blessing*: the prettiest child; ringlets, dimples, *et cetera*. But his next canvas must an image of a loving mother-and-child and most respectfully done. Will you be our lady? No? Oh, such beguiling modesty! Then will you oblige him for the sake of Holy Father? At the end of our days is it not for the glory of Mother Church that any honest Catholic labours? You say yes? I'm much relieved! Rest assured it'll be most efficiently done. That is, if we now make our way, and expeditiously, to my Master's studio he can meet you and render your image in charcoal. The child? No, no, I think not: the noise is certain to be too much for my Master; I'm sure the dear will be quite safe with your maid and my Master may then preserve his creative reverie. He'll imagine a child for you to hold, Viscontessa, and do so with professional ease.'

Stephen persuades; she complies. Of course she does; it's preordained; written in the stars. If the prize seems too easily won I beg you to remember that Stephen's blessed with both physical charms and a manner of speaking that much appeals to the female species. In short, she's ready to be charmed ... and he charms her most readily.

She died well enough, when one considers the pain she endured. Later, I hope you uncovered her remains in the grounds of the Villa Borghese. No? Then you and your men have been dreadfully lax; in fact, cruelly idle. You must now make things right and recover her without further delay, Cavaliere: gather up her bones with all due respect and return them to her family. Allow her husband to assuage his grief. That said I hear he already speaks quite openly of marrying again. Send word to her Roman house without further delay, Cavaliere. Have a heart.

ASPHALTUM.

A suitable colour for the work in hand comes to mind: Asphaltum. In its purest form it derives from bitumen. Pulverize a cinder of quality Asphaltum, mix with it half an ounce of sugar of lead, half a pound of the calx, then add a drying oil, all prepared in a litharge. Expose this to a hot fire and see it melt like butter. When it comes to the boil remove it immediately from the heat and place in a glass vessel suspended by a thread in a bath of cooling water. This will produce an excellent colour for shadows. It takes a glaze well, boasts great longevity, and isn't susceptible to cracking.

The seventeenth day of January
in the Year of Our Lord 1776.

Today's feast day of Saint Anthony the Egyptian, desert father of monks and patron saint of infectious diseases. A true ascetic, he pitted his wits against satyr and centaur, but wrote nothing in praise of himself or his struggle. Modesty is the mark of a noble heart; note how I sing like a canary in praise of mine!

Cavaliere,

A little advice: leave the poor to their own devices. They're most accomplished self-annihilators, culling themselves in a great variety of methods ranging from suicide and murder to the acquisition of diseases of both the sudden and wasting varieties. Their apocalypse, ridding the world of their blight, is best achieved by simply leaving them to themselves.

The educated, noble classes are an entirely different case, having many and varied means at their disposal to prolong life by avoiding deadly calamity. It's a truly rare thing for the *nobilitas* to willingly delete themselves; they're stubborn, clever, often well read and rightly fearful of what lies in wait for them beyond the veil. Even in time of war they rise up, up above the fog and rely on the common folk to perish in their stead.

In time I will redress this imbalance, sending a delegation drawn from the privileged classes into Hades ahead of their time. I'm a cutter of threads.

The Sixth Labour of Heracles:
the Stymphalian Birds.

Rome plays host to a colourful—and well moneyed—community of Sardinian exiles. Their grandparents set down roots in this fair city after their home was wrested from them by Vittorio Amedeo di Savoia and their grievances have grown legion. Ah! But you've already encountered one such castaway in the person of Tenente Colonello Cesare Guastalla. Remember him?

Generations have come and gone since they first nested within these city walls and now their descendants display no yearning for their ancestral home. But despite their good fortune are they quiescent? No, not a whit: forgive their radical politics if you can, turn a blind eye to their wayward thinking if you're so inclined, but why must they insist on driving the city mad with their arrogant posturing, agitating and petty politicking? They intrigue over cups of wine, rant indiscriminately and always far too loud. They do nothing to redeem themselves, taking out loans and defaulting on their repayment. They have no integrity; they are the worst kind of men. To rid Rome of even one such pariah is an act of mercy; they're useless and will be neither mourned, nor even much missed.

Venture with me once again into Antiquity to the court of an angry and humiliated King Eurystheus. This time he dispatched Heracles to dispose of a swarm of malicious, odious birds flocking on the shores of Lake Stymphalia. I call them "birds", but they flapped along on wings of brass, jabbing metal beaks, devouring human flesh and shedding poisonous dung wherever they went.

Without doubt they were Sardinian birds. Do you see where I'm going with this, Cavaliere? This scourge, these pets of Ares God of War, could launch deadly metal feathers from their wings, but Heracles had the better of them in the blink of an eye. He startled them into flight and shot them down to earth with his mighty bow. Take note that while Stephen's certainly no

Heracles he has practiced archery from childhood and is thoroughly competent.

Now then, how to scare up our own Sardinian birds? We set our scene as true as we can to Greek legend. Stephen and I, sympathetic to our fellow expatriates, insist that Monsieur Yves and his sister Adèle—a pretty young thing, albeit cursed with an irritating, high-pitched giggle—come with us to take the air and enjoy the splendid views. The sun shines down on our adventure and a mile or two along the Via Ostiense, liberated from the city's narrow confines, swarming populace and overpowering aromas, we rest awhile beside the Abbey of the Three Fountains where it's said that Saint Paul encountered the headsman's blade.

Later, we come to the Lago di Bracciano. 'I've arranged for a little health-giving amusement to occupy us before luncheon,' say I, with calculated jollity. 'See! Over there lie our targets and here we have archery-bows. We shall mimic the peasant archers of Stephen's native land and shoot arrows for sport. No, no, it's in fact quite easy,

Adèle, even with my twisted hand. You only have to try and you'll see that I'm right. Feel the lightness of the bow! Here, Yves; here, Adèle. Take up your weapons and Stephen will instruct you in their use; he's most proficient. Don't be distracted when you see him holding the bow in his right hand; he's left-handed like myself. See! It's not so difficult and with the next arrow you might even strike the target. Have a little faith, Adèle, I pray! There! I declare a certain kill, Yves, or at least a mortal wound. Now then, you two young things hurry along: retrieve your spent arrows while Stephen and I make ready for our turn in the lists.'

They obediently trot off, chattering like children, to where the straw targets are fixed to a tree. They search out their arrows, but imagine their alarm when it becomes suddenly—and most painfully—clear to them that it's they who are, in fact, the true quarry. My disability confounds my aim and I only succeed in winging the lad with my first shaft—he's much quicker on his feet and less bewildered than his sister—but

Stephen downs them both with alacrity, one after the other with only two arrows! Joy in his success momentarily overwhelms him. I feel a distinct pang of jealousy: Stephen's exceeding me in many things these days. Their sufferings are eased with the aid of a hunting knife; we're never cruel.

HARTSHORN.

For this part of the Work I'll employ Hartshorn. Here's the process: crush sufficient dried deer antler and mix it with an oil of the requisite quality. Long ago I despatched the noble beast, their former owner, with my favourite hunting piece (a Farmer & Galton; I'll trust nothing less). He was a most handsome fellow and his crowning glory, once rendered, has assisted me in my Work since that day. He's achieved a singular form of immortality.

The tenth day of February in the year of Our Lord 1776.

Today's the feast day of Saint Scholastica, patron saint of convulsive children, whose name also invokes protection against the ravages of storm and rain. The divine Scholastica had the briefest of careers. First, she summoned up the tempest to provoke the Godly conversation for which she so fervently yearned, but then caught a chill from the damp. The chill grew into a fever from which she promptly died. It's said that her spirit flew heavenward in the form of a dove.

How sweet.

Cavaliere,

My present situation is mine by choice. I daily exercise my right to free will, God's ultimate condescension to mankind. But that same precious, hard-fought liberty is also His means of keeping us tight in harness to wallow in a sea of permanent guilt. God knows our vast capacity for error. So, being doomed from the second I drew my first breath, I resolved early in life to exploit the benefits of human frailty to their utmost. The usual consequence of exercising this freedom is hellfire and damnation: so I was heading in that direction the moment I awoke to the world. Choice, but no real choice at all.

I'm an Artist of repute. I move in elevated circles. I swim through society's polite soup by right. I rise above the crowd; I'm *nobilitas*. With thanks to Stephen I also enjoy freedom from the attentions of the justiciars.

Who other than you within my circle, Cavaliere, could so much as imagine the deeds of which I'm capable? You plan to discover my secret passions. My initiation into the Dark Arts came from Paracelsus' spirit. My familiar, Kabalos, came to me from him.

Paracelsus. I'd entirely forgotten about him until this moment. Doubtless you'd like to know how Kabalos came to be in my service—*or perhaps I in his!*—so ask the Master himself. He's on the Other Side, of course, so you must engage the services of a competent *magus*. Oh, and be careful he doesn't summon up a *maleficus* in error: therein lies a world of sad mischief and grave danger.

Paracelsus, or Philippus Theophrastus Aureolus Bombastus von Hohenheim, was a countryman of mine, did you know? Bombast by name and bombast by nature, he declared to the world that he had the better of Celsus, the Greek writer, physician and enemy of Christianity. Preposterous, but *Para*celsus was also a much venerated master of the alchemical arts and therefore commands my devotion.

Here's how I sold my soul. I entered my edge-place and named a sin. I elected Ira (that is, Wrath), simply because this was the first one to enter my head. I drew a sharp knife across the palm of my hand. Blood flowed from the wound. I dipped a pen into the blood and wrote "Ira" upon a strip of thin vellum, wrapped the scroll around the waist of a glass flask and inserted three fingers, including the bloodied, into the neck. I watched, entranced, as a single drop of my life fluid fell into the water, quickly turning it viscous and black. A gust of sulphur filled the room. I withdrew my fingers, moved across the room and soon a hideous figure dragged itself upward through the neck of the flask, sucking at the air like a drowning man, growing ever larger as it emerged from its confines. First came its claw-like hands and then a terrible face. The thing then set on to gabber at me in a language I didn't understand.

I became fearful. I confess it freely. It was too much to bear. I begged him to retreat immediately from whence he came, but the creature fixed me with such a stare and then answered in a low, grating voice—*this time in my native German!*—that the spell, once uttered, could never be repealed! Not without the interference of a competent priest with bell, book and candle. In this way I summoned Kabalos into the world, but now he doesn't appear willing to return from whence he came. I fear he's become overfond of *terra firma*.

The Seventh Labour of Heracles:
the Cretan Bull.

For his seventh penitence Heracles was sent out in pursuit of the infamous Minotaur, who'd acquired the inconvenient habit of devouring fourteen young men and women each and every year. Once liberated from the confines of the maze the beast wrought havoc the length and breadth of the isle of Crete. Our indomitable hero strangled the hellish creature with his bare hands, rendered it unconscious and carried it to Athens. There, Eurystheus vowed to sacrifice it to the goddess Hera, but Hera so loathed Heracles that she refused the offering! The Minotaur was set free once again, this time to wander into Marathon and continue his reign of terror.

And so to business: where to find a man suited to the part of my fearsome bull? Rome provides a ready solution to my quandary: on the riverfront any desire can be assuaged. Luca advertises no surname, perhaps to add a little more lustre to an already ruthless reputation. He's a thoroughgoing bravo, notorious murderer and infamous extortionist. A Sardinian, susceptible to flattery, and therein lies his fatal weakness.

Stephen baits his hook with the promise of a substantial fee in return for the removal of a certain patrician, knowing very well that Luca holds men of his ilk in utter contempt. He loathes the idleness of politicians, their arrogance and especially their intrusion into his private dealings. His obsession's further inflamed by Stephan's reports of—*our entirely fictitious*—politicos' evil deeds.

Further persuaded by alcohol—including, of course, certain additives as recommended by Paracelsus—he declares his intention to accept the contract, but only if allowed to fulfil it entirely gratis. Later the same evening he lies in wait for his quarry, his vision and reactions becoming evermore hesitant, not realising that the true quarry is, in fact, himself. Watching his head begin to loll Stephen and I prepare a ligature for our Minotaur's neck, but even in his reduced state it takes every ounce of our strength to make an end of him. No release into the wilds of Marathon for this Cretan Bull: he's ignominiously pitched into the river.

The river, yes. It flows languorously at this time of year, replete and murky, concealing who knows what. I'll employ a good deal of my Naples Yellow to reflect its surly look.

NAPLES YELLOW.

Lead Antimoniate is highly poisonous, but I offer it as a truly excellent substitute for Lead-tin Yellow. It will, however, produce a less intense colour, in fact a rather pale hue, yet I find it appealing, much akin to Flake White. To its credit it dries quickly, but on the debit side stands its extreme toxicity. This, unless carefully administered, will lay you flat in a trice; so do not breathe in its dust if you value your life and good health.

The eighteenth day of March
in the year of Our Lord 1776.

Today's the feast day of Saint Cyril of Jerusalem. A theologian of great repute, Cyril stole precious ecclesiastical goods then sold them in order to feed the poor. Despite having the noblest of motives he still suffered painfully for his generosity once his thefts were discovered. The Vatican is no compassionate master.

The Eighth Labour of Heracles:
the Diomedian Mares.

I'm destitute with tiredness. The responsibility of the Work weighs heavy on my shoulders. Fortunately, I'm recovering from my infirmity. Unfortunately, I fear its resurgence with every waking hour and remain intractably left handed, albeit now with only a modest impairment. I wonder if I'll be so condemned forever: will I never be restored *in dextera*? And what, I wonder, might all this signify? There are many *sinistra* associations. Is this some Godly punishment? If so, for what? Do I shame society? No! I'm its most loyal upholder; I'm its fortress and strong defender.

The four Diomedian Mares were magnificent; feral, man-eating horses held in the stables of the giant Diomedes, a harsh master and a soldier of great renown having fought in the Trojan War. He was one of the chosen few concealed within the immense wooden horse dragged into the city by the witless Trojans. Heracles tethered

Diomede's Mares to a bronze manger, leaving a youth to stand guard over them while he fought and slew the giant with his mighty axe. The luckless boy, however, was devoured by his charges—the Mares. Infuriated, grieving, Heracles fed Diomedes' body to his own beasts, then bound the Mares' mouths tight shut for the sake of safety and drove them away to King Eurystheus who dedicated them to Hera, most likely to irritate Heracles afresh.

The Barone Benardo Biaggio speaks with a lisp. He's a patrician, born of a much-respected noble line, but is disarmingly modest for all that. Had he possessed a disagreeable nature, what followed would have been so much easier. His stable of horses is trained to fight with teeth and hooves. They're the mightiest of beasts; the fastest and most fearsome in the whole peninsula and the Barone loves them more than his own life. This at least lends a little poetry to what follows.

    I've seen Kabalos at work and his skill matches that of the deftest Roman butcher. He's quick and fastidious, flensing, quartering and butchering the Barone in a matter of minutes. His flesh we feed to the pigs, his bones we roast, crush into powder and mix with the contents of the feed bins from which his warhorses will soon have their breakfast. All this before their master's even missed. Come morning the place will erupt in hullabaloo as the absent Barone's sought high and low. Nothing will be found. Not a scrap.

VERMILLION.

For a serviceable Vermillion use Cinnabar. According to Theophrastus, natural Cinnabar was once dislodged from inaccessible cliffs by the shooting up of arrows. Its opaque, pure red is the heaviest pigment I employ to produce good, durable flesh tones. But don't be tempted to adulterate it with cheap Red Lead, which will render it too dark. Standards, standards!

**The twenty-fourth day of April
in the year of Our Lord 1776.**

Today's the feast day of the martyred Saint Fidelis of Sigmaringen. Fidelis, the patron of hair shirts, refused to renounce the True Faith even after Calvinist soldiers hacked off his left leg. Why such brutality? Simply this: to punish him for journeying through their lands in search of converts to Catholicism.

The Ninth Labour of Heracles:
Hippolyta's Belt.

Ares, God of War, presented his daughter Hippolyta Queen of the Amazons, with a marvellous girdle. King Eurystheus coveted her treasure, desiring to make a present of it to his own daughter Admeta, and the ever-penitent Heracles was dispatched to retrieve it. At first the negotiations went well, but then a rumour took hold that Heracles was intent on the capture of the Amazonian Queen herself, at which point her fearsome warriors rushed to protect their sovereign. Thinking himself betrayed, Heracles killed Hippolyta with a single blow, ripped the girdle from her lifeless body and set sail, his gory trophy held aloft and blood running from his hands.

And whom shall I find to play Hippolyta's part? Who indeed? Imagine my delight when I discover a small band of outrageous refugee women, come here to Rome from the islands of Tavolara and Corsica. What an accommodating city this is! So cosmopolitan, embracing all the worlds' waifs and strays! Corsica's the place that in 1755 unwisely granted women the right to vote, but then wisely revoked the statute by corrigendum in 1769 when the ever-sensible French took possession of the place. However, it seems that a patriotic fire still smoulders in their souls, fanned by the scratchings of Antoine Condorcet, the fantasies of Olympe des Gouges and the rantings of that ridiculous American harpy Lydia Taft. In any case, here lurks a community of women most vocal in pursuit of their "democratic rights" who would raise up a veritable army of radical Amazons to wage cruel revolution. What follows, Cavaliere, is almost poetic.

Beneath the guise of a sympathetic, attentive man of letters Stephen sets out on his hunt. A prime example of their kind is close-courted and, Cavaliere, you may complete her story from her remains, which you will find hidden in those pretty little gardens above the Spanish Steps.

I'm well aware of the fictitious claims that are finding their way to your ear, but they are so much confetti and products of vain delusion. You have in your hands a detailed, reliable account of her murder together with certain other details—affixed herewith—to which spurious claimants couldn't possibly lay claim: *i.e.* her lips being laced together with twine. I also removed her ring finger and carry it with me now by way of a *memento mori*. She was once Maria Lucia Bertoleoni and if you require more evidence her possessions, including her clothing, can be found hidden behind the wooden chest in my rooms. Would you be so kind as to return them to her family on the island of Tavolara? I think she hails from the little town of La Maddalena and I've an idea that her family's well known in those parts. You should be able to locate them easily enough.

SMALT.

You might detect the liberal use of another of my favoured pigments in this Work: Smalt. Nota Bene—Roast a good deal of cobalt ore with other ingredients to create a frit, using much the same method for Egyptian Blue. Smalt is otherwise known as "Alexandrian", "Pompeian", "Pozzuoli" or "Vestorian Blue". It's most often applied to ceramics and used in the work of sign painters, but I find it excellent if in the mixing the handler's adroit and things are well ordered. Its effect does not emerge alla prima, so you must persist: repaint the area several times with diligence to achieve the proper effect.

**The second day of May
in the year of Our Lord 1776.**

*Today's the feast day of Saint Athanasius the
Apostolic of Alexandria, that famous vanquisher of
heretics. In fact, he was an inestimable coward
and died peacefully in his bed.*

The Tenth Labour of Heracles:
Geryon's Cattle.

Geryon, a fearsome giant, bestrode the island of Erytheia—Red Island of the Sunset. He had three heads, each bearing a human face, three bodies and six arms. His constant companion was the monstrous, two-headed hound Orthrus and together they stood sentinel over a great herd of magnificent red cattle. The indomitable Heracles traversed the Libyan wastes to despatch them both with a massive olivewood club and his bow. I think he might have evened the odds in their favour a little, don't you think? Heracles, you mean-spirited fellow! Hardly sporting, but our hero had a penchant for making an end of his opponents by unusual means. Geryon, beneath his three armoured helmets, behind three stout shields and hefting three sharp spears, waged a mighty battle until Heracles abruptly concluded the contest by shooting him through the forehead with an arrow, the tip of which he'd previously, and most cleverly, dipped in the venomous blood of the Lernæan Hydra. Remember the

Hydra, Cavaliere? Unsporting perhaps: a deception and profoundly unworthy, but then Heracles inflicted yet more humiliation on his victim by tearing Geryon's body into three parts.

How, then, to meet such a challenge and yet demonstrate my philanthropic sentiments for the people of Rome? It proves easy enough in the end: the governance of this fair city lies firmly in the grip of that same band of brigands so despised by Luca, my dead Minotaur. By "brigands" I mean the political classes; the debauched, sin-steeped, corrupt and corrupting over-class of this fair city. Its functionaries have learned nothing from the Greeks; they trample down the principles of democracy and are, to a man his woman, debased beyond redemption.

Giacomo Bruneschi, Niccolò Rao and Rodolphe Bernino hold lucrative stipends in the service of our Holy Father. Pope Pius VI, the current Bishop of Rome, once suffered as a man in the form of the man Giovanni Angelo Braschi after which he was elevated and named, in a mystical puff of white smoke, as the descendant of Saint Paul and God's worldly representative on earth. Within the precincts of il Vaticano our less-than-divine, politicking triad have made themselves disgustingly rich, spreading their largesse here and there, but always in one selfish cause or another, the shameless bellygods. What's more, I'm sure none of them would shed a tear for the inhabitants of the city's poorer quarters. In the stews, envy of our trio and their kind is rife. Venom flows freely, a river in constant spate. Leaflets have been printed to castigate these men, much in the style of the Parisian *libelles* that so grievously plagued Queen Marie Antoinette, but my three-headed Geryon won't be so mourned. Be sure of that, Cavaliere.

Now here's a worthy challenge: this is the first occasion upon which my Work requires the destruction of three souls within a single heartbeat. Not for the first time I'm glad that Stephen's joined to me. He plays the part of a visiting nobleman and we hold a sumptuous dinner in honour of Signores Bruneschi, Rao and Bernino. They arrive, oozing grace and condescension, ostensibly to discuss lucrative trading agreements for fine spices, good quality paper and virgin girls out of Africa. We've barely progressed beyond small talk when Paracelsus' infusion makes its presence known. All three pass meekly, with a little encouragement and a minimum of fuss, gentlemen at last after lives of self-serving thievery, face down in their soup. Each body's divided into three parts: head, torso and legs. To sow confusion the parts are confused and three composite bodies, all friends together, are distributed around the Colle Palatino. What amusement!

LAPIS LAZULI.

For my next creation I will employ a quantity of Lapis Lazuli: "Azzuro Oltremarino" (Blue from beyond the Sea), or "Lazuline Blue"—beautiful names, don't you think? Counted among the most costly of painting materials, a cerulific is magicked up by firmly grinding the Lapis Lazuli, then purifying it in a complex process to extract it from the grey, modest-looking rock within which particles and veins of Lapis Lazuli lie tangled up. Handled in the right manner a tint of nigh-uniform hue can be produced. This is a much sought-after commodity for an Artist. It was once found in Assyrian and Babylonian relics, employed as a decorative or precious stone. Can this be Theophrastus' and Pliny's sapphire? I think it is.

We play an elaborate game, you and I. I make a calculated assumption that your failure to prevent the deaths is weighing heavily on you and you're beginning to feel a little responsible for them. Perhaps this creeping sense of desperation has caused you to plunge head first into the classics and, in particular, the Labours of Heracles. You propose to steal a march on me, anticipating my next action and, if you're in good time, prevent it.

You might also have dredged up Apollodorus of Athens' account of Heracles' deeds in the hope of more revelation. Do you recall my suggestion that you make a foray into academe, that day you stood before my first canvas? You were reluctant to take advice from one such as I—a common flaw among your ilk. Too proud, too proud and blighted by a disease common in your class: laziness bred of lofty arrogance and over dependence on the labour of others. But if I'm mistaken, and you've indeed been hard at your studies, then you'll know that there were originally only supposed to be *ten* Labours. King Eurystheus, however, decided that the death of the Hydra wouldn't count towards the total. Furthermore, because Iolaus had assisted Heracles in the Augean Stables, this task was also declared null and void! Two further Labours therefore ensued. Heracles, the proudest of men, was irate.

**The thirteenth day of June
in the year of Our Lord 1776.**

Today's the feast day of Saint Anthony of Padua, the patron saint of finding things. Oh, and also barren women. He was well versed in the scriptures and a renowned speaker, neither of which prevented his agonising death from ergotism. He longed for martyrdom most fervently, but only really succeeded in having the illness that caused his end named after him as "Saint Anthony's Fire".

The Eleventh Labour of Heracles:
the Apples of the Hesperides.

For his penultimate Labour Heracles was dispatched once again into the domain of his habitual enemy Hera. Her orchard lay in the far west and was permanently festooned with a lush crop of golden apples that, if eaten, would bestow immortality. Attending the orchard were the Hesperides, a triad of beautiful nymphs: Aegle, Arethusa and Hesperia, who commonly debased themselves by feasting on the apples. The jealous Hera appointed Ladon, the hundred-headed, insomniac dragon, to guard her orchard, but our Heracles entered, slew the creature and made good his escape with trophies in hand.

Had Hera-the-incontinent been able to contain her envy I might have depicted the three nymphs at the centre of this canvas, but no: it must be Heracles doing battle with yet another fearsome beast. A little tedious perhaps, but at least this next Work will necessitate the eradication of a worldly Ladon.

Picture my joy when a suitable candidate presents himself. Despite his high office the Cardinale Giovanni Cosimo is as ungodly a man as ever walked the earth; a devil in the service of the most Godly of patrons—the Archbishop of Fiorenze, Francesco Gaetano Incontri. You know him, I think. Cosimo had the good fortune to be appointed Prefect for the Congregation of Indulgences and Relics and is also the most devastatingly clever man I've ever encountered. He exploits his station with consummate skill. In parts of Europe the Catholic faith is suppressed, but despite this there are many Catholics hiding in the creases of the map. I count myself among them despite my antipathy towards priests. I—and those like me—exist where the True Faith's obscured from the light of day by Protestant nihilists. Where the articles of the True Faith are proscribed, honest men and women cling fast to the small things of comfort. Wherever desperation is found, cunning men, only too willing to exploit it, will seldom be far behind.

The Cardinale Giovanni Cosimo portrays himself, with no redeeming display of humility, as divinely appointed; placed on earth to address the needs of those embarked on one or another spiritual quest. The pious are his eager congregation, so potential victims abound—suggestible, guileless folk. He makes faithful copies of the genuine relics under his control and sells them to unscrupulous merchants. These villains then extract money from gullible pilgrims, providing divine wonders such as fragments of the True Cross, phials of the desiccated blood of saints, remnants of the cassock said to have been worn by Pope Clement XIV on his deathbed and sundry other travesties. Incidentally, this last "relic" is doubly false: Clement died of either *1.* a long-standing scorbutic and hæmorrhoidal affliction or *2.*, as vouchsafed by the more excitable witnesses, a poison administered by the Jesuit Brotherhood. In either case, Clement died in a stinking mess of soiled bedclothes and not in his cassock. More than this, the Cardinale has sold so many fragments of the True Cross that I estimate the original must surely have been at least a hundred feet tall and considerably broader than a barn; a very large barn.

The Cardinale has grown prodigiously wealthy and now here he is, come to Rome for a private audience with il Papa. The faithful Stephen seeks him out in the guise of a prosperous English merchant. Cosimo's only too happy to be entertained with a sumptuous dinner in the course of which he's promised a little "business" from the English Catholics. Having conspicuously enjoyed the wine the Cardinale becomes voluble. In fact, he proves to be an atrocious show-off, brim-full of his oh-so-many conspicuous achievements. So flagrant is he that my reluctance to lay hands upon a man of the cloth, even one so degenerate, diminishes by the minute until in my mind's eye his throat's already a fountain, opened up from ear to ear. He has by his side a bag of samples with which he hopes to tempt Stephen. Here are Hera's apples: the keys to eternal life for no one at all, and utter damnation for the Cardinale Giovanni Cosimo in particular.

Once we are done with him his remains are displayed, for all to see, crucified beside the Via Appia, his "relics" stuffed inside his mouth and sundry other orifices. Is this too sordid for your taste, Cavaliere? Then study the finished piece and see all this entirely justified. Oh, and do you appreciate my clever use of Masticote?

MASTICOTE.

To create a Masticote, or Lead-tin Yellow, apply the usual method, but be aware that it's deeper, or more pinkish in hue than litharge; it'll also blacken in time and alter more rapidly still if exposed to direct sunlight. Cennini remarked that its tint can also be injured if too vigorously ground up. Italian writers referred to it as "Giallorino", "Giallolino" and "Giallolino de Fiandra".

Incidentally, the Consul Appius Claudius had the Via Appia constructed in 312 BC. Did you know that? I heartily recommend an energetic walk along its length, but not in the heat of a summer; in Spring or Autumn the temperature and the light are infinitely more agreeable come early evening.

**The twentieth day of July
in the year of Our Lord 1776.**

Today's the feast day of Saint Apollinaris of Syria, patron saint of epileptics and the gout-afflicted. Beaten wherever he chose to preach, he eventually met his death at the blade of a sword, which I'm sure would at least be preferable to the ravages of gout.

The Twelfth Labour of Heracles:
the Great Dog Cerberus.

What a thoroughgoing dullard you are! I'd hoped you would prove a worthier adversary than this! From across the street I witness the violence with which your men beat down the door to my apartment, though it stood innocently unlocked and unbolted. If only they'd thought to try the latch first. I watch from under the brim of my hat as you lead them inside only to discover me gone. Departed with me are the paraphernalia of my calling and every shred of the evidence you so fervently seek. You lose my scent, Cavaliere, and know it. But take heart; cling fast to the lingering hope that I'm vaguely misplaced rather than precisely lost. I hope you'll not give up. After all, you possess a truly dogged nature and earnestly desire to see me hanged. Dogged, yes. I imagine you a spirited hunting-dog, perhaps a bloodhound or deerhound. No: more likely a watery-eyed, ageing Spaniel.

The time has come at last. Stephen and I flee the city incognito, departing in the direction of Fiorenze; Florence;

the place of your forefathers, Cavaliere, and home to your ever-loving family.

You were present at the *protasis*, Cavaliere, fumbled your way through the prolonged *epitasis*, and now the time of *catastrophe* is upon you. But you must pursue us with alacrity, so I urge you on. Heracles' twelfth and final Labour was to bring back Cerberus from his station guarding the doors to Hades. A simple enough task, you might think, for had not Heracles already overcome Cerburus' brother Orthrus? Or had a lust for revenge turned Cerberus more ferocious than ever? Agreed he did have fifty heads, or was it a hundred? No matter, for this was quite the most perilous of Heracles' tasks.

Our hero entered the Underworld at Tanærum, presented himself before Hades' throne and asked for permission to take Cerberus away with him. Consent was granted, but only as long as Heracles promised not to harm the beast in any way. So, he wrestled with the slavering Cerberus until he reduced the great dog to a state of abject submission. Good boy!

So where am I to find my guard dog? Bark, Cerberus and I'll drag you back from the Realm of the Dead. I already see one hound snapping at my heels, Cavaliere, but do you foresee what I have in mind? No, I think not. Study the finished Work to know with certainty that our efforts, yours and mine together Cavaliere, were well spent. Oh, and do you appreciate my clever use of Verdigris?

VERDIGRIS.

The "Green of Greece", Viride Aeris, possesses the same grey-green, or bluish patina that forms on ageing copper. When blended with oil it will convert to black and tend to impermanence, being much affected by the atmosphere. It can be purified using vinegar and Da Vinci advised that if not promptly varnished one may remove it easily with a damp sponge, especially in humid weather.

A nugget of information has come to me regarding your late father, the esteemed Cavaliere Eriditario <u>Vittorio</u> di Credico. An eminent fellow, sure enough, what did you know of the man beneath the fine gowns, position and magnificent accomplishments? What of his substance? Was he a doting father? You'll know this, but what you may not know is that when outside the polite society of the family mansion the Cavaliere Vittorio was utterly ruthless. He took a perverse delight in the eradication of his enemies. He crushed the last influence of the Medicis, who've never loved the name of di Credico, and continuously sought the favour of the Grand Dukes of Lorraine. Your father was their faithful hound in Fiorenze and as such was richly rewarded; raised up to become the City's Justiciar. How much of that di Credico bile did he inflict on the populace? Be sure he served his masters well. You, Cavaliere, have enjoyed the manifold fruits of his labours; wherever he sowed, you have reaped in abundance. The sins of the fathers ...

What follows is made so much easier by the atmosphere of celebration that erupts in Florence at this time of year. In the Piazza di Santa Croce they play *Calcio Storico Fiorentino*: a ludicrous, and riotous ballgame featuring teams drawn from the four quarters of the city. The jollity draws the entire populace into the city centre, leaving us at liberty to play a game of our own devising; a magical diversion of disappearance and reappearance; a dramatic sleight of hand. Unnoticed, we enter the di Credico family crypt and bundle up the noisome remains—still moist, reeking—of the Cavaliere di Credico the Elder. This part becomes detached from the next despite his being only recently deceased. It has been unseasonably warm.

We carry his chaos in a sack through the streets. Later that night, with hooks, nails and wires, we affix up his foul smelling, corrupted, decaying corpse to the gates of the di Credico family mansion on the Via Appolonia and witness the hullaballoo at a safe distance. Fear of disease and horror at his stink makes them all reluctant to touch the corpse, so he's on display for a good while. Thus inspired I sketch. I mix my colours. The contract with Milord is all but fulfilled, now the denouement beckons.

We agree on all things, but Stephen's work is complete and he prepares—I think most reluctantly—for his return to England. I will continue alone and bring things to their conclusion. We agree to rendezvous at the Golden Lion Coach-house before proceeding to Enderby. I confess to be a little relieved at his departure—the suspicion grows within me that he covets my station, reputation and Work for himself. That can never be.

With Stephen gone I feel certain everything will now proceed to plan: after such provocation you're bound to pursue us to Florence, Cavaliere. Be tempted, be persuaded, but will you smoke my ultimate, dark intent? It may well be that you've read a little, perhaps even delved into Peisandros of Rhodes and construed this last undertaking to be my final Labour. If so, you're about to be proven wrong.

On the heels of the recent hiatus a lengthy peace descends; what follows will demand patience and planning. It's possible, Cavaliere, that during the fallow days preceding my final endeavour you'll have presumed me either dead or disappeared, and breathe a secret, deep sigh of relief. But then I'll prove myself very much alive. In fact, I've been an industrious, busy little bee. You see, the di Credicos Elder and Younger are not the only members of your esteemed family with whom I intend to have dealings; I have it in mind to seek out your daughter; the beautiful Sophia. Oh, I've already seen her, but only from afar. She's utterly beautiful. A butterfly. I long to feel the brush of her wings upon my skin. She's somehow ... "other"; far above this tawdry, stinking world you and I inhabit, Cavaliere: elevated, angelic and yearning to be cut free from her earthly limitations.

With her assistance the Work will achieve its completion; the entirety of the poem set down for you, Cavaliere Ereditario di Credico. When your soldiers stamp rhythmically along il Ponte Vecchio, up to and through my door, you'll discover three things: first, the powders from which I mix my colours, their odour still permeating the chamber, but never quite masking that faint whiff of sulphur. Second, you'll uncover *The Maere* on the easel, beneath a scarlet satin cloth, beside a century of burned-out candles. Third, you'll find Sophia's carriage-cloak of deep midnight blue, which you'll no doubt recognise immediately. A heart-sink, dread realisation will then penetrate your soul: a sense of your butterfly lying dead below a closed-up window.

Why Sophia? Put simply, she's your daughter. Her name is all I need to make my poem rhyme. The thread of your daughter's life is woven through the essential last stanza. All that follows is inevitable. Find comfort in that.

The last item you'll need to complete our story is this diary. Here's my confession: my affidavit for you to place before the city's judiciary. It will come to you in time, but is this honest confession, or work of fiction? In any case, do with it what you will, but you'll never lay a hand upon my person, Cavaliere: I'm mist: everywhere ... and suddenly nowhere at all. But should you ever come close to me, move to trap my essence within a bell jar, you'll fail. No noose for me: Paracelsus' final gift to me is perfected for precisely such an eventuality: my chemical remedy for life. This ingenious mixture of powders is the last measure of bliss I'll enjoy before my final descent. I'll have plenty of company about me in the afterlife; I've dispatched many others before me and they'll doubtless have much to discuss with me. But it's you and not I who ought to properly fear immortality, Cavaliere: history prefers the strong, no matter how evil their deeds.

**Il Ponte Vecchio, Fiorenze,
on the twenty-seventh day
of August in the year of Our Lord 1776.**

*Today's the feast day of Saint Monica of
Hippo, a Berber out of the African deserts and
mother to Augustine who would, in time, be
sanctified himself.*

The Thirteenth and Final Labour of
Aloysius Amerigo Beade.

Here we are, come to our *denouement* at last. I'll revenge my death while yet alive. You, the Cavaliere di Credico, are a bloodhound with my scent in its nostrils. You seek me out, yearning to see me hanged up by the neck, but I'll never be stretched and thrown down dead, head lolling, into some anonymous lime-pit. That's an end for fools and I'm certainly no fool. Justice will fail you: all you imagine you hold in your grip is will-o-the-wisp. You'll learn soon enough that the only thing left to you is revenge, and in that you stand to lose as much as I.

But how dare you, ignoramus, seek to hound me to death? You stand, feet apart, hands on hips, square in my path. Feel the breadth, depth and height of my fury. I'll revenge myself on you before you can do me any harm. Follow me back to London if you will, then on to Kent. There, find me transferring my Work onto the walls of Milord's Long-room.

Press me and I'll deny every charge you lay at my door and with many aggrieved protestations. I'll shout to the world that my presence in Rome and Florence were merely coincidental. These jottings? Why, simply a work of fiction based on recent goings-on in Rome and Florence. Mere frippery; a creative diversion. Were the murders not widely published? I'm an avid reader. You'll be able to prove nothing; I'm untouchable. In any case, I have no fear of death, only a terror of ignominy, and that makes me nigh on invincible; a Heracles.

Enough! Today's a most auspicious day. Today we venerate Santa Monica of Hippo, though quite why we revere her as a saint when the sum total of her achievements was to squeeze out into the world one such as he! In a mass of piss, shit and blood she gave issue to that infamous debaucher, fornicator and Manichæist priest from Tagaste, is all quite beyond me. Her errant son stumbled down his private Damascus Road, but then, from under the carapace of a superbly flawed man there emerged, butterfly-from-chrysalis, the hallowed Saint Augustine: Aurelius Augustinius Hipponensis.

Santa Monica was a Berber. Did you know that? It therefore follows, Cavaliere, that by just one remove the progenitor of the esteemed Augustinian Order was part Arab and this, in its turn, betrays the presence of a little pagan desert sand coursing through the veins of Mother Church. Priceless! I do appreciate such a prime joke.

After stalking Sophia about the town for a week I discover that your daughter's a creature of habit. This makes her vulnerable: I know where she will be and at what time, so all I have to do is place myself in her way. My pretext? I return a stolen handkerchief she thinks long since lost and engage her in a little innocuous conversation:

'Di Credico, you say? Why, I believe I might know your father!'

'Surely not!'

'He and I met at the home of my patron, Lord Halebroke.'

'I'm astonished! What a coincidence! "Patron", you say? Father counts Lord Halebroke a friend, although he is an Englishman. Oh, can you forgive me?'

I can; I do, and easily, being thoroughly unEnglish myself. I reveal that I'm an artist, likewise foreign and therefore at liberty to complement her beauty with impunity. *Nota Bene*—It's perfectly acceptable for the Artist, under the concealment of professional interest, to comment on such details. That said, beautiful girls are usually vain to the core and will assiduously soak up any and all compliments.

That your daughter's beautiful—and unsettlingly so—be of no doubt. She displays a sense of decorum and impeccable manners, but then there's that stray frond of hair that falls, uncontrolled, at her left temple. She twists it between thumb and forefinger when confused or pensive. I tell her this: since arriving in Fiorenze I've planned to render a simple, charming little picture of a girl asleep.

Beautiful in its simplicity. *Maiden, Safe in the Arms of Somnus* will be its title.

'What do you think, Signorina? Will you pose for me? There's a surfeit of girls to be found in Florence, all with adequate physical appeal, but never one so perfect as you.'

She overcomes her discomfort and agrees, but not for my sake: it appears that we share the same ambition: she hopes *Maiden, Safe in the Arms of Somnus* will stir the blood of her paramour. She's chin deep in her private passion! Did you know you'd raised a vixen in your hen coup, Cavaliere? And in season to boot! I'll give this undertaking a secret title: *The Maere*, after the incubus I imagine squatting upon her chest.

Not even you, Cavaliere, will immediately appreciate the significance of all this, so allow me to explain. In old English, the mongrel language of my adoptive home, my incubus might well have been named *Mære* and from that I construe my title. You may also like to search out the word "nightmare" in Johnson's *Dictionary* where you'll find *"mara, a spirit that, in the heathen mythology, was related to torment or suffocate sleepers. A morbid oppression in the night, resembling the pressure of weight upon the breast."*

Herewith another piece of the jigsaw: discover the *Maera*, the eastern Lord of Misfortune, Sin, Destruction and Death, who sorely tested the Buddha ... and lost. Today, in a monumental fit of devilish pique at his defeat, the *Maera* exacts his revenge, testing us all to destruction. The *Maera* loathes Man; he blinds us, tempts our sensual desires and will ruin us utterly if he can. He's cunning, scheming to capture the souls of men and bind up all Creation in chains. We're besieged, day and night, *Maera* longs for a world in which venality holds sway, false conscience reigns eternal and bloody war is waged without end.

My incubus sits here beside me as I write. "Kabalos" simply means "rogue", but his other names are legion. In the primitive cultures he's known as "spriggan", "bogle", "sprite", "goblin" and "gnome". He goes by other names, in many different tongues, across manifold separate histories. He may very well sound harmless, but how much is revealed in a name? A great deal, as it happens.

To get about the city he straddles a horse. I say "horse", but in truth his sorry-looking runt's a poor imitation of that noble creature. Kabalos once told me, an impish grin smeared across his face, from pointy ear to ear, that his four-legged corruption answers to the name of "Pegasus"! What a sumptuous irony! Look deep into and then across the world's mythologies and you'll discover the horse to be mystically bound up with the elemental powers of wind, storm, fire, wave, running water and life. Oh, and also death. Return to the Buddha to learn that he departed this earth astride a beautiful, white steed. Incidentally, the horse is also—and so deliciously—associated with sexual energy, impetuous desire ... and lust. Look closely at *The Maere*, Cavaliere, and you'll see that my Pegasus is a rather unremarkable chestnut nag and is, more importantly, entirely blind. You might construe something else from that, if you have the wit and intelligence.

We form a solemn contract—your legalistic mind will doubtless approve of that, Cavaliere —and Sophia Amelia di Credico comes to me, bearing a bag of silver coins, shortly after midnight, and begs me to paint her image without delay. Up to this point the evening has been all-but wasted, enduring an interminable opera seria—I entirely forget the title—so the prospect of plunging myself into the Work promises welcome relief. Her proposition's simple enough: to paint the famous virgin Sophia Amelia di Credico in utter secrecy.

    My purpose is self-evident, but what of Sophia's? She intends to gift the portrait to her would-be lover, doubtless to induce sighs and much clasping to his hairless chest an image of a body utterly forbidden him. You say you weren't aware of this? Of course you were: her lover was once sent away and declared thoroughly unsuitable by you, the esteemed Cavaliere di Credico!

How contemptible! Have you no heart? But in spite of your opposition Sophia and her paramour most certainly do love each other. Or is it the very proscription of their attachment that's fanned the flames of their rebellious ardour? My, how you have misjudged your daughter, Cavaliere: under that serene surface she's wilful and utterly determined. In fact, you seem to know precious little of human nature; you'd rather speak than observe and you've not yet learned to listen.

There's only one possible way to proceed and I'm brim-full of stipulations: the Work must remain utterly confidential and no one, not even the lowliest servant, may be allowed to learn where and when our meetings will take place. *In the event of any contravention*, say I, *the canvas will be entirely burned up*. She accepts all this readily, perhaps believing it an artist's foible—*in truth, who knows?*—but I think she also discovers a certain frisson in our whisperings. Eve, when forbidden a particular apple, deprived Man of his rightful eternity in Paradise, so in the grander scheme of things this is small beer.

And you brought all this about! What splendid irony! You, Cavaliere, Sophia's noble father, would never allow her to venture out of doors except in the company of some drab, thoroughly tedious chaperone, but if the Work's to proceed as planned she must be entirely alone in my company. The night hours are preferred—candlelight is so evocative.

Sophia pleads her case. I feign demurral, yet in my mind I'm already reaching out for brush and palette. She writes to me the next day. I study her letter over and over again, closer and closer still until ... Eureka! There, concealed beneath the florid script, a secret message lies tucked away. There, between the petals of a delicate flower I sniff out the hidden scent of her desire. I'm gifted in that way; as a spaniel is to a whiff of partridge, so am I to a woman's illicit perfume. I accept the commission.

Of course I do.

We begin our clandestine meetings. The beautiful Sophia steals her way out into the darkest part of the night, shrouded in a carriage cloak of midnight blue. My muse, a blindfold drawn tight over her eyes, is guided to my door by Kabalos. They move in the shadows so as not to betray themselves to the rare night watchman not already in his cups. They approach my rooms by a different and evermore circuitous route each night, so should my plan go awry she'll be incapable of betraying me. Her cloak laid aside, Kabalos arranges her posture on the couch with touching gentleness and care—recall what manner of creature he is! He moves a supple limb a little this way and a tress of glossy hair the slightest touch over there. He twitches the folds of her shift just so and I remark that the attitude of her body's set the same, in fact identical by every possible measure, to that arrived at in the previous sitting. He replies that he knows precisely how the finished portrait must be, carrying an image of it in his head every living minute, awake and asleep. In this way he achieves his tender miracle night, after night, after night.

The mood I strive for is best served with a careful application of my finest Peachstone Black. Study it, Cavaliere, and solely by candlelight if you can. See how what you first thought patches of plain black are shot through with shade and subtlety. There's a new world lying in wait for you there: a second canvas to tease the mind.

PEACHSTONE BLACK.

To achieve something above the commonplace black rendered from iron gall, search out good charcoal, soot, or lampblack, peachwood prunings or, better still, crushed and roasted peachstones. Laid on thick it's very dark; apply in sufficient quantity it will suck down all the light in the room, drawing you into the heart of the painting.

One hundred candles are lit; five points placed. At each sitting Kabalos goes a touch further, lingering just a little longer over his ministrations, drifting leathery, taloned fingers across the youthful form beneath the linen. One night he allows a claw to stray, just a little, brushing lightly across a nubile breast. Sophia doesn't move, but I detect a splash of ruby colour rush to her lips; a blush spring unbidden to her cheeks; a betrayal in her sudden intake of breath. The harlot! Disappointment rises; gorge in my throat.

This is hopeless! My subject must remain utterly still; unshifting and not altering her colour with abandon. She must be as unmoving and pale as tonight's gibbous moon. I decide to administer the lightest dose of poppy and other, subtle things intended to both immobilise the body and temper her youthful urges.

The next night and for those to follow Sophia implores me to increase the dose, just a little more each time, reckless of the dangers of partaking too often and too enthusiastically of Paracelcus' concoction. I'm powerless to resist. Under his ministry Sophia remains perfectly still until, as the dawn light appears and the last candle gutters out, there comes the time for her to leave. I'm utterly spent; all my life force daubed, reckless, across the canvas. Yet the Work progresses well. Her shape? Abandoned to my inspection. Her demeanour? Simply abandoned. Delectable. I've surpassed myself.

I'm exhausted unto death, but do I then find solace in sleep? No: my devotion to Michelangelo calls me forth onto Fiorenze's streets. Many years ago I declared myself willing to die in the service of the Work, so a little fatigue matters not a whit. Everything in its season: to Michelangelo the head and heart, to Kabalos the viscera.

I declare the portrait finished, but Kabalos purses his puffy lips and points to its lack of ... something: its quintessence. Then Sophia asks for a still greater measure of Paracelsus' philtre and, once she's drunk deeply from the flask, she falls into a dreamless sleep. Kabalos goes about his careful work, arranging her shift as precisely as before, but this time he clambers up onto her supine body to stare with intensity at the rise and fall of her breast and the subtle, pulsing vein in her throat. At that very moment—*what revelation!*—I suddenly perceive every deficiency in the canvas before me and set to work with supernatural vigour. Kabalos squats in his place all the while and Pegasus stretches his neck around the curtain, whickering his excitement. Later, as I set down my brushes at last, one hundred candles dead and my exhaustion absolute, the incubus turns to me and grates ...

'She's gone from you now. Gone from you ... and gathered to me.'

At last I can to finish the Work. Through dawn and into the day I paint until it's at last complete: *The Maere*, the Thirteenth Labour of Aloysius Amerigo Beade. I transform the portrait from what is into what must be. There, for the span of this eternity sits Kabalos, captured at the very moment he feels Sophia's last, fluttering, breath under his feet and then the gentle ... subsiding ... cadence ... ... of ... ... her ... ... pulse.

Once Kabalos has completed his ministrations her earthly remains are disposed of with alacrity, wary first of the discovery of a certain empty room, in a certain house on the Via Appolonia in which the bedsheets lie shockingly unruffled. Then, allowing for the inevitable, unpleasant effects of the summer heat on all things corporeal a measure of haste is required. Fortunately, my rooms straddle one of the Ponte Vecchio's vaulting arches and a convenient trapdoor yields ready access to the river Arno swirling far below the span. But do not despair, Cavaliere: the image of your daughter, Sophia Amelia di Credico, will be with us forever; her youthful beauty rendered timeless, incorruptible, while her mortality drifts gently away, downriver as far as the deep, deep Tyrrhenian Sea.

Finis.

Epilogue.

Cavaliere Eriditario Riccardo Francesco di Credico.

Sir,
According to the instructions of the Court I forward herewith various documents and an account of certain events to you, having been summoned in my official capacity to the deathbed of Mr. A.A. Beade, Artist, at the Golden Lion Coaching-house, Spate, on the fourteenth day of November 1776.

Mr. Beade had arrived by way of the London coach late in the afternoon of the previous day and before the great storm of 13th November set in. Admitted by the Patron he was accompanied by a good deal of baggage including a good many canvases, his being an artist, and *en route* to attend upon Lord Eustace Halebroke at his estate of Enderby.

The Patron will also attest that Mr. Beade was greatly agitated from the first and his clothes somewhat dishevelled. He retired immediately to his rooms, having exchanged very few words with anyone there present.

He had attended the Golden Lion on several previous occasions yet had never before drawn down such attention at himself, being a thoroughly well regarded gentleman and most generous in his manner and conversation. Yet in this last visit he might well have been mute, so reserved and nervous was he. He requested a light supper to be carried up to his room and after that he retired very early, leaving certain instruction that (1) he was not to be disturbed under any circumstance, and (2) that another gentleman, either friend or associate, would be arriving after him and instructed a room to be made ready for him. The same room lay undisturbed at the time of my inspection.

Thereafter, accounts are confusion, for the Chambermaid will swear that Mr. Beade arrived later, <u>after</u> the great storm had set in, and came into the place very wet and demanding that a fire be built up in the Best Room so he might dry and warm himself through.

The next morning the cadaver was discovered by the same Chambermaid. The contents of his room were discovered to be in considerable disarray; the aforesaid light supper lay untouched. The Maid remains much distressed at the time of writing.

I observed the deceased: a middle-aged man lying prostrate with arms outstretched and legs together in a semblance of faithful supplication. His remains appear to have been arranged thus *post mortem* and with considerable care. The Patron of the Coaching-house had covered his face with a bedsheet beneath which the deceased's expression was in *rictus*, in the way of a man in great terror or pain. His greyed hair was dishevelled and I detected traces of blood under the fingernails of his left hand. Resulting from some long standing infirmity the right hand was much wasted and the fingers contorted into a tightened fist. Palpating the man's chest I observed several of his ribs to have been broken and the cavity thereunder quite stove in and liquefied. I am therefore convinced, both from observance of the physical evidence and vouchsafing the statements of the several witnesses, that the Victim had been the object of a sustained violence.

Testimonies gathered from the Arthur Giles, Patron of the place, his Potboy, Chambermaid and sundry others bear witness to loud disturbances in the early hours of that morning which, by every account, emanated from the Victim's room. Unfortunately, the clamour was universally ignored and assumed to be "private" in nature, the place being clearly no stranger to vulgarity and bawdiness. The Potboy, an uncommonly astute little fellow despite his lack of learning, was convinced that he had heard shouting on the part of the Deceased and that of a companion thus far unidentified. The Boy was surprised to learn that Mr. Beade was most certainly alone in his room at the time in question.

The same voices were also heard by a second witness who described them as follows: one deep and grating and the other higher in pitch and much distressed, most likely that of the Victim. The source of the second voice remains a mystery as no one save the Deceased was seen to either enter or leave the room. Furthermore, the Patron has assured me that the premises are securely locked and bolted throughout the night from long established habit.

Certain facts of the case I am unable to explain. Upon visiting Mr. Beade's destination, the home of Lord Eustace Halebroke <u>subsequent</u> to the events described above, I can report that the Long-room at Enderby now exhibits a full suite of twelve *tableaux* depicting the heroic deeds of the Greek Hercules. They may be freely inspected at your Lordship's pleasure. Lord Halebroke is adamant that the deceased Artist was himself responsible for their execution, although this is obviously quite impossible, the Victim having been discovered dead several days previously.

A number of the original letters are unintelligible to the untrained eye and I therefore append for you convenience several transcriptions previously rendered for the use of the Court. It is apparent to me from my experience in such matters that authorship of said letters, despite all of them bearing his signature, or something like it, is in fact attributable to two individuals, the first drawn up by a shake-handed individual and the latter by a steady-handed scribe. Many annotations had also been appended to earlier documents by this same second, and more resolute, hand.

I have omitted, again for the sake of expediency, parts of the collection in which the first Author scribbled most wildly and rendered a series of pictograms (meanings undetermined). All canvases (save one, entitled *The Maere*) and sketchings were absent from the room, their present location unknown.

>   Your Servant.
>   Edward Ferrier, Justice of the Peace
>   This nineteenth day of October 1776.